THE BONSAI TREE

THE BONSAI TREE

MEIRA CHAND

First published in 1983 by John Murray (Publishers) Ltd

This new edition published by Marshall Cavendish Editions in 2018
An imprint of Marshall Cavendish International

Other Marshall Cavendish Offices:
Marshall Cavendish Corporation. 99 White Plains Road, Tarrytown NY 10591-9001, USA • Marshall Cavendish International (Thailand) Co Ltd. 253 Asoke, 12th Flr, Sukhumvit 21 Road, Klongtoey Nua, Wattana, Bangkok 10110, Thailand • Marshall Cavendish (Malaysia) Sdn Bhd, Times Subang, Lot 46, Subang Hi-Tech Industrial Park, Batu Tiga, 40000 Shah Alam, Selangor Darul Ehsan, Malaysia

National Library Board, Singapore Cataloguing-in-Publication Data

Name(s): Chand, Meira.
Title: The bonsai tree / Meira Chand.
Description: Singapore: Marshall Cavendish Editions, [2018] | First published: John Murray (Publishers) Ltd, 1983.
Identifier(s): OCN 1039233205 | ISBN 978-981-48-2823-9 (paperback)
Subject(s): LCSH: British--Japan--Fiction.
Classification: DDC 823.914--dc23

Printed in Singapore

Cover design by Lorraine Aw

To

OSYTH LEESTON

with thanks

1

There were sounds now at last. Kate went to the window, peering out into the dark, at the lamp that glowed above the tall roofed entrance gate. It was opened by Itsuko's chauffeur and her mother-in-law appeared. In the sphere of light Kate could see each speck of snow on Itsuko's sculptured hair and the soft fox fur around her neck. She placed a hand on the join of kimono at her knee beneath her short silk coat. Jun came through the gate behind her and opened an umbrella above his mother. They hurried forward and were soon hidden by a wing of the house. There was the sound of the front door sliding open, their voices and Fumi's welcoming greeting. Earlier, Kate had seen Yoko arrive and her voice now joined Fumi's. Kate continued to stand at the window, on the same few inches of bare polished board where she spent so much of each day, staring out through the pane of clear glass inserted for her in the frosted window. It was six weeks since she arrived in Japan.

She should have gone down to greet them, as was expected, as she always did. Instead today she waited, but Jun did not come up to see her. He had left at five that morning for an early flight to Tokyo. Left before she even awoke and returned in the afternoon, going straight to the office in Osaka, and coming home only now with his mother. She listened for his foot on the stairs, wanting some moments alone with him before the evening began. Today of all days. She lingered a few moments more, but there was no sound. At last she turned to the door, knowing she could delay no longer, that they would be waiting for her downstairs.

They were seated round the table when she entered the room, Jun, his mother Itsuko and the two aunts, Fumi and Yoko. Old Hirata-*san*, the maid, hurried in with hot *sake* jars on a tray. On the table two empty containers already awaited replenishment. There must always be alcohol when Yoko visited. It was suspected she consumed unhealthy amounts, for often on the phone to Itsuko in the evening, her voice was a gentle slur and inclined to weak emotion. She looked up with a smile at Kate and patted the cushion between herself and Jun. He nodded to Kate in a preoccupied way as she sat down awkwardly on the floor, a hand on her belly, for the child kicked suddenly inside her.

The meal was already laid on the low table, in many small delicate dishes. A meal of yellow-tail fish and crab, hot bean paste soup with needle mushrooms, steaming hot rice, pickles and a salad of roots and sesame seeds. The food and the language were still difficult for her, even after a year of marriage.

'Oh,' said Itsuko, kneeling primly, her eyes upon Kate across the table. 'I thought you were out.'

'Out?' Kate puzzled, meeting her mother-in-law's gaze.

'You were not at the door to greet us. What else could I presume?' Itsuko replied. 'It is our custom you should be there, as you know. It is a matter of etiquette, a matter of manners. Were you not well?'

Kate hesitated, looking at her husband, willing him to speak.

'You know how tired she is, Mother. She's not yet used to our ways.' Jun defended her but Kate could not forget he had not come upstairs to find her, today of all days.

'Not used? She must *get* used. We have a position to maintain.' Itsuko was in her sourest mood. A problem at the office had upset her whole day.

'Gently, gently,' Yoko cautioned. 'She comes from another world. I know. I have travelled. There, I have seen a daughter-in-law waited upon by her mother-in-law.' She meant to help but her sister's face grew sharp as granite and Yoko was not displeased. In the past she too had often been victim of Itsuko's imperiousness. The *sake* swirled pleasantly in her.

'Oh what a pretty bracelet.' Yoko took Kate's wrist and examined an Indian bangle.

From where she knelt at the end of the table Fumi darted quick anxious looks, hating the strain between them all. She bustled suddenly beside the maid, making room upon the table for yet another small dish.

'Will you pour us some *sake*?' Itsuko demanded more kindly, holding out her tiny cup.

'Of course.' Kate rose clumsily to her knees, anxious to please. The small jar was hot in her hands, the cup beneath it seemed little bigger than a thimble. She steadied her fingers about it, but the liquor spilt over her hands and onto a plate of pickles.

'Oh,' said Itsuko. 'Careful, careful.' Vexation cracked her face. Could Kate do nothing right? She was all sincerity, all spontaneity. Itsuko thought of the girl she had picked to be Jun's wife, the daughter of a Diet member, an old and noble family. Tentatively, she had even made the first enquiries through a go-between, and found them well received. She thought of the face of that young girl, passive and touching, a face of delicacy and reticence. What an asset such a girl would have been. How much she would have furthered Itsuko's innermost ambition. And in the house she would have known her duties, known her place. Instead, she had acquired Kate who moved about so clumsily in both the world of tables and emotions. She could not even keep the traditional slippers on her feet. Often, Itsuko heard in the corridor the skidding of a piece of footwear. Or upon the bare and upright stairs a falling thump, and the woman's low fierce words, 'Christ. Damn it.'

'Don't worry,' Yoko comforted, pulling her legs to the side beneath her, leaning an elbow on the table, chin upon her hand. 'I don't like that variety of pickle, the *sake* will improve it. We'll add more soy too.' Picking up the jug she dribbled a dark stream of sauce over the limp, green pickles.

She enjoyed baiting Itsuko, and felt guilty too for the severity with which Itsuko treated Kate. She herself had liked Kate immediately, and welcomed her into their family. Everybody she knew had commented immediately on Kate's quiet beauty. She had a slim, long-legged grace, and had no need for even the light make-up she wore, for her skin was fine. The sharp boning of her face set off the intelligence of her wide-set grey eyes. Long, thick red hair and a flair with clothes made most women envy her, and the men always clustered about her; but she appeared unaware of these qualities, and did not seem to notice the looks she drew.

If she had been a Japanese, thought Yoko, she would have allowed herself to feel jealous. Instead she stared at Kate in admiring curiosity, Her expression was never still, but reflected each feeling in a way quite alien to Yoko. It was fascinating to watch her. She reminded Yoko of a French actress she had seen in a recent film. Yoko sighed enviously and smiled as she caught Kate's eye.

'You too, Yoko, are greatly lacking in your etiquette. It does not become you. And at your age,' Itsuko admonished. Yoko shrugged and added more soy sauce to the pickle. She did not care. She had long ago gone beyond all limits.

Why could Yoko not set a better example, Itsuko wondered. Look at her, leaning over the table, slurring her vowels, her expression lax and vulgar like a common bar girl. Yes. She must admit it. For this was the image that came to mind nowadays with Yoko. And she did not wish to think about it but she suspected there were lovers. However, she had long since washed her hands of Yoko, long since made it clear to the world that this younger sister was no part of the family honour. But it made Itsuko mad to see such delight with a foreign niece-in-law. No doubt Yoko liked the image. Curiosity, if not acceptance, was in her lazy eyes.

Itsuko gazed at Kate bitterly. In the old days a mother-in-law had a daughter-in-law on trial and sent her home if proved unsuitable. *Sent her home.* Or even later dissolved the marriage, perhaps overruling a son's objection. Even now some divorces were initiated not by a husband, but by his mother. But this was rare. For nowadays all was lost identity, all was interest in the foreign, a breaking with traditional ties, the old wine was in new bottles, the old concepts remodelled to modern trends. Just so had she acquired the daughter-in-law who now sat across the table. She could not forgive Jun. She should have married him off before he went to England.

The worst shock had been to see that Kate was already with child. It had been a surprise when she first saw Kate at the airport, hanging onto Jun's arm, waving, smiling across the barriers. Itsuko had felt quite faint, she had not known Kate was pregnant. And when they came out, Kate had moved forward, smiling, pushing her cheek against Itsuko in embrace. Such a thing had never happened to her. She had been unprepared for the distress that swept through her powerfully. She had pulled away in a short, sharp jerk and a gasp of rattled breath. Jun bowed deeply in respect while saying something low to Kate, so that she drew back, her smile fading to a blush. Even now Itsuko shuddered to remember the moment of physical contact, such gaucherie and garrulity. These were the ways of foreign lands. These were ways she did not know and never would if she could help it.

But tonight they all annoyed her. *The woman.* She could think of her as nothing more, could not in her mind give her the endearment of a name. *She* who now competed for her son's affection, an affection Itsuko took as her own right; the small change, the only loving return from a long and solitary marriage. And that highly unrepentant son, fussing round his wife, weak-willed, directed by her, hurrying always to spread oil on troubled waters. Troubled waters. She would give him troubled waters. And Fumi, dowdy, befuddled, indistinguishable sometimes from the maid. And did Fumi think that Itsuko had not noticed those little smiles and whispered encouragements passed surreptitiously to Kate. God alone knew what sentimental waffling she imparted to Kate through their house-bound days, while Itsuko supported them, worked for them, navigated the world of industry from her office desk. And Yoko. And Yoko? What could be said of Yoko? What had it come to, their grand family name? These few tatters round this table? Only she, it seemed, had inherited the iron vision that had always propelled her father and her grandfather.

Itsuko stared at the small blue chrysanthemum printed in the bottom of her empty cup. For the first time in her life she dare not look into the future, nor predict it as she always had. It was enough to drive her, like Yoko, to a bottle in the evening. Instead, she thrust out to Kate once more the thimble-sized *sake* cup.

Kate sat back when the round of small cups were refilled, trembling still, the heat stirring then pulsing through her. Suddenly the child began to turn, quickening in her like silver on a tooth, its heart moving against her own. So that she put a hand to her belly as if to hold it still. Across the table Itsuko's face was stripped and brutal in its bitterness. She was expected, Kate knew, to prove loyalty to her mother-in-law, satisfying her every wish. Such obedience here was virtue. If a wife and a mother both were drowning, explained a proverb, a son should save his mother; wives were two a penny. In the old days at a family meal a daughter-in-law must sit by the side of the hearth where the smoke blew in her eyes. In this modern age these attitudes withdrew to shadows, but a residue remained. These things she knew, she tried her best, but ignorance and sometimes pride cut rents into each day.

She had met Jun first at one of Paula's parties. When she arrived the room had been a crowd of strange faces to her. Paula's husband, Pete, was talking animatedly to an attentive Japanese, he waved and called her to him, introducing her immediately.

'Kate Scott, Jun Nagai. Kate is a friend of Paula's and works at the same interpreting agency. An accomplished lady, university graduate, speaks Spanish, French and German.' He gave her a congratulatory pat on the shoulder. 'And Jun is from Japan, although we didn't know him when we lived there. He came to me here to buy dyestuffs; he's in England to study British textile methods. Jun's from a very old family who owns spinning mills in Japan.' Pete soon turned away, to talk to other guests.

The Baileys were American. Pete worked for a multi-national chemical company that trundled him around the world with his family, to spread the sale of detergents and paints. Paula, who had been a teacher of modern European languages before her marriage, was working while in London at the same interpreting agency where Kate was also employed. The Baileys were in their third year in London, after a five-year posting in Japan. They had loved Japan, Paula told Kate, and hoped to have another posting there.

Jun found a couple of empty seats and they sat down together. On a small table beside them stood a painted lacquer box. As a point of conversation Kate asked Jun its use, knowing it came from Japan. The Baileys' were avid collectors. Japanese antiques and ornamental objects, bought on their previous posting to Japan, adorned their apartment. Retrieved from the dust of curio shops and flea markets, *tansu* chests, woodblock prints, chinaware and lacquerware were forced in the room to be mere decorations. A brazier became a plant stand, a candlestick a lamp, part of a painted sliding door hung framed upon a wall.

'It's a *kai-oki*, a box to store the shells used in an ancient game. Later the Portuguese introduced Western cards in the sixteenth century.' He spoke slowly in good English, and she was struck by the quality of his voice.

'Shells?' she queried.

'A species of clam; the shells were beautifully decorated and must be matched together. In some shells half a poem was written, and the other half in its mate. But it was all a long time ago, you know.' He smiled at her rapt expression.

'Modern Japan is another world.' He got up to refill her glass and she watched him cross the room, aware of his interest in her. As he made his way back to her with fresh drinks, pushing his way determinedly between the groups of effervescent people, she observed the expression on his face as he concentrated on the glasses in his hands. He frowned as someone jogged his elbow, slopping drink onto his thumb. His purposeful passage through the room seemed out of place in the general frivolity and facetious conversations. He sat down again with an apologetic smile, wiping his wet hand with a handkerchief.

'And what are all these pictures?' she asked after he had settled, continuing their conversation, pointing to the Baileys' collection of woodblock prints. Jun nodded, eager to explain.

'Those of the big, fat men, are old portraits of sumo wrestlers. The others are all *Kabuki* actors.'

Kate listened, the alien words conjuring up an unknowable world, wise and esoteric. She felt already a little removed from the gusto of the room, and protective of Jun's special sensibility before the gaucherie of the crowd. His expression held at all times a formality and reserve.

He was not a big man, slightly taller than her, but this did not distract from his masculinity, there was a suppleness about him that was almost feline. His skin was smooth, his hair thick and sleek; there was the scent of cigarettes and certainty about him. Even his thoughts, Kate felt, must not be haphazard like her own, but exact and polished, laid out in neat piles in his head, for he produced them with an air of such certainty. 'You're an oriental enigma,' she later told him, laughing. But in the beginning it had been impossible to know what he might be thinking, until she learned to read him.

At the table Itsuko sipped her *sake*, and Kate took care not to meet her eyes. It seemed impossible now to think that only six weeks before these sisters about the table had been no more to Kate than names upon a sheet of letter paper. Now she called them family, and felt as a piece of soft fruit in their hands, to be bitten by them to the core.

It was difficult to reconcile the common blood that flowed between the sisters. Neither chalk nor cheese, nor night and day could adequately explain the differences between the elder two who lived together in the old family house, bereft of men. Both were widows, both bound within society to be no more than shadows of the dead. But Itsuko, had the boldness and the arrogance to step outside her circle. She continued to run her husband's business, silencing male dissent, and soon placed herself at the head of the family. Such audacity in a woman was unheard of; the headship of a family was the heritage of men. But Itsuko held shares and power, she was the eldest of three daughters in a family without a male heir. As was customary in such cases, her husband was adopted, to inherit the family business. It had been he who came like a bride to live in his in-laws' house. His own name was struck from his family register, and he took that of his wife. Itsuko had never respected these admissions of want and weakness. For what able, well-established man would accept such a loss of male prestige in return for prospective security? Of course, although impoverished he was of desirable descent; he was not just anybody; the marriage had brought connections. In public Itsuko produced the deferences demanded, but in her own mind she felt superior to her husband.

She could never forget she was a Nagai, nor the feeling that her life, unlike other women's, was not to be tempered by circumspection. In a house of women she had never known the traditional subservience to brothers, never had to knuckle beneath a mother-in-law. Early in life she saw a path marked out for herself as if she were a body; these were strange thoughts in the head of a woman.

But she had still to wait for her husband's death. She seized that moment to succeed to the headship of the family until her son, Jun, came of age. Senior male relatives of branch families were powerless before the fact of shares and her will; they helped her for a while. Ambition was solid as her own flesh, before her directions took clear shapes and consolidated strength. She refused the passive place of widow and her allotment as a woman, she stepped in every way far beyond her role. She was shrewd and cunning, she had vision and charm and an essential business acumen. In the twenty years since her husband's death, she had moulded the Nagai Spinning Mills from a large into a prominent concern. Her name was known beyond spheres of work, for she was all but alone in Japan's industrial world as a powerful, active businesswoman. 'It is only,' she had said, 'until my son comes of age.' But the words did no more than wet her lips and dissolved again to the shapelessness that was then all the years ahead. Now Jun was thirty-one, impatient for his future.

There was much less to be said of Fumi. Accepting and effacing with hair as short and coarse as badger fur, she began sometimes to knit a garment that had no destination, that might begin as a jumper and end as a scarf. Fumi, in widowhood, accepting and effacing, receded to her proper place, as a "cold rice relative", at the beck and call of the family and mute to all decisions. She became her sister's housekeeper and closed her eyes to that other life that had deprived her of a husband and at different times, two children. Her daughter had died in infancy, and her son had been killed in a motorcycle accident at the age of nineteen. The unrelenting destiny that left her so plain and homely refused to endow her life with more than a minimum of warmth. Her husband's fortunes had dwindled quickly into debt and soon he took his life. These sorrows shattered her last assumptions and left her as she was. The past was mirrored in her untidy outline, compassion was solid in her face.

Yoko was the baby, twenty years her sister's junior, born late in life to elderly parents. She saw her sisters' marriages from her mother's knee. Her eyes still held in their waywardness the results of early spoiling, and a certain exclusion through age from the centre of the family. She had always lived in a world of her own, believing the difference in years placed her in another era; she was a modern woman. Her independent spirit made it difficult to arrange the most suitable marriages. She offended, deliberately, any number of go-betweens, and when pressed to attend *miai* meetings with designated bachelors, spoke or acted commonly or afterwards found a birthmark, baggy trousers, or a tendency to drunkenness in her suitors that no one else had noticed. In spite of an exclusively feminine education, she found at sixteen an unlikely romance with the son of the gardener. This was soon smothered by the family in shame, and fear of leaks that might wreck her chances of a future marriage.

The family could never see it was the instinctive rebellion in Yoko that aborted each attempt to marry her.

When their parents died in a car crash, Itsuko continued the campaign to get Yoko married. At last she consented, with stubborn bad grace, to marry the son of an old business acquaintance, but almost at once she took a lover. Her husband divorced her immediately. All she did was heave a sigh of relief and refuse to feel the stigma. Such shame, such gossip, such wantonness was a slur upon the good name of her husband's family. Yoko did not care, she had a worldly new status, financial means, and was a woman of her time. She began to earn her own living, cashing in a small reserve of talent and numerous connections. She became first a designer in a fashion firm and then left to start her own boutique. Now she had a thriving business of her own, and lived by herself in a flat in Kobe. Itsuko disowned her, but time, the proverbial healer, mellowed the wound. There was talk upon the telephone, and sometimes now a visit. At forty, Yoko was beautiful still in her selfish, languid way, with wine-dyed hair and the fineness of Itsuko's skin and features in broader bones and jaw.

Once, thought Kate, looking across the table, her mother-in-law had been a passive bud, mild and charming, and submissive. Kate had seen old photographs that showed a face where dreams and gentle secrets were sewn up deep inside.

The child quickened in Kate once again, she held her breath and closed her eyes upon its strange, determined presence, turning in her like imprisoned vines. Perhaps this child would be the link across histories and mentalities, would change things in touching, innocent ways. She willed and prayed it, pushing tears away. She felt ill with natural causes.

Jun touched her gently. He survived each meal in silence, ignoring her before his mother. She felt mean to blame him for her difficulties. It was not his fault. He lay between his mother and herself like a frail, slat bridge across a chasm.

She remembered the Baileys' mixed response to the news of her engagement to Jun.

'We're so happy for you.' Paula had hugged her, but in the same breath expressed caution. 'It is not an easy society to marry into.'

'The Baileys don't think I should marry you.' She told Jun later.

'Kate. Believe me. Everything will be all right.' He took her hand, clasping it firmly. It was as if in a choppy sea, someone had thrown her a rope, and she grasped it gladly.

They married, and in one breathless year she saw her certainties fulfilled and her doubts dissolve. She made a beginning with the language, taking lessons at an institute and acquired a taste for the cuisine. She achieved a deft use of chopsticks and spoke of the meaning of inner space in Japanese art and architecture. In a luxury flat above Holland Park, with a view of lawns and chestnut trees and some swans upon a lake, she seemed with ease to possess Japan already in the palm of her hand. Nothing prepared her for the reality.

She looked up to find Fumi's eyes upon her and smiled. Aunt Fumi nodded, fussing with some stubborn wool caught about a button. Kind as always, she differed from her worldly sisters in character and also in looks, for as Itsuko had decided, she was indistinguishable from the maid. Her life had been drained of happiness, yet there was no bitterness in her face. She smiled encouragingly to Kate.

Jun drank his soup, bowl to his face, his eyes safe within its circle. Kate wanted to turn to him, to remind him of today, for clearly, he had forgotten. She did not eat much, nervously mashing the thick wedge of fish with her chopsticks, picking small flakes from a bone. She had no appetite, yet dare not leave it, already she felt Itsuko marking the mess on her plate. The silence was broken only by the faint wheeze of the oil stove glowing within its corner, the slurp of soup and the knock of chopsticks on a bowl. They concentrated on the meal, Itsuko's will reflected on them all.

Kate moved uncomfortably on her cushion. She had been five months with the child when she arrived, and almost at once her own clumsy body seemed to turn against her and refused to manipulate the sitting and sleeping on floors, the deep baths, the narrow corridors and small rooms. And her own solidity terrified her, growing as she watched, unstoppable. She shifted heavily, moving an aching leg. She had never complained, managing to sit as required through each meal but day by day as her weight increased she new how clumsy she appeared, in a way she had never known before.

Jun put down his chopsticks. His mother's eyes stung like nettles in his face. He ignored her and turned to Kate.

'You can't sit like that. Wait. I know what to do.' He got up and left the room.

'Yes. Yes.' Fumi read his thoughts and hurried after him.

Itsuko continued with her soup in silence, the bowl before her face, her chopsticks guiding the stalks of mushrooms into her mouth, ignoring Kate. Soon Jun and Fumi returned with the soft, yellow backrest from Fumi's room, and pushed it beneath Kate's cushion.

'Now stretch your legs out straight beneath the table. Better?' Jun asked. He pressed her shoulder, bending to her, although he knew her eyes sought out the love between them. Their return to Japan was much worse than he had feared it would be.

'That's better,' nodded Kate. But it was the closeness of his concern and hand as much as any backrest. It seemed less painful that he had forgotten today. Soon they would be alone; she would not allow her disappointment to weigh upon them. She placed a hand gratefully on Jun's knee beneath the table.

Itsuko's eyes narrowed. From the end of the table Fumi darted a harassed glance at her sister, and was at pains to refill the *sake* cups before Kate could be admonished. Yoko leaned on the table, refusing to be part of the moment. Her sister's predilections had nothing to do with her. She had long since washed her hands of Itsuko's affairs. Jun did not speak, sitting again like a statue, guilt and anger at his mother raging within him. He did not dare to look at Kate, the meal continued slowly.

'We must hurry,' Itsuko spoke suddenly, looking across at Jun. 'Don't forget, we have an appointment, they will be waiting for us.' Jun nodded silently and continued with his meal.

'Out? You're going out?' Kate asked dismayed.

'Yes, there are things to discuss with a tenant of my mother's.' He had told her nothing of his plans, not wanting to disappoint her. He was waiting for the outcome of this evening before he approached his mother.

Fumi's kindness was far away, unable to help, and the words burst out Kate.

'Do you have to? Do you have to go?'

'Yes.' He spoke sharply, in an effort to appease Itsuko. Kate did not understand this strategy, she could not see the more gentleness Itsuko sensed, the more distaste stirred within her. Kate's eyes filled with tears, Jun looked away, hating himself.

'Will you be long? Will you be late?' Her voice was low and flat.

'I don't know, possibly. Don't wait up. I have no idea when we might be back.' He forced himself to say it with cruel detachment. Itsuko granted her approval with a small, firm nod. A tear trickled from Kate's eyes.

'What's the matter now?' he frowned. Afterwards he would explain why he had to do this.

'I haven't seen you today. You went out at five this morning. Today was our wedding anniversary.'

She had not meant to say it, but fatigue was a weight she could no longer carry. Now she had said it she knew it did not really matter, that it had little to do with her tears.

How could he have forgotten? Jun cursed himself and saw sudden light in Itsuko's eyes. He could keep up the pretence no longer, and took Kate's hand apologetically, Tears spilled down Kate's face.

Itsuko looked on in disgust at such overt demonstrativeness. She did not glance in Kate's direction but returned with dainty expertise to a last piece of ginger pickle. Jun took no notice of Kate's tears, he stood up and left the room. Itsuko nodded her approval, laid her chopsticks on their rest, her rice bowl cleaned of each single grain, and followed him from the table. Soon there was the sound of the front door closing behind them.

Kate tried to sleep, but the waterfall disturbed her, rushing as always through each night, and through each day behind the clack of the bamboo water-pipe in the garden. The contraption filled and emptied ingeniously, with a sharp noise that scared away birds. A January cold consumed the dark, polished surfaces of old wood in the large, bare room. A space that smelled astringently, of smooth rush mats, padded tight, of mothballs in a chest of drawers and the fumes of the small oil stove. She wished for a chair, but there were none. She was not yet used to a life on her knees, to the sudden drop of eye levels and the altering of perspectives. She heard Yoko depart, and later Fumi brought hot chocolate and biscuits as an offering of comfort. Kate lay in the bed of thick quilts spread upon the floor, and listened to the waterfall. Falling, falling without end, its sound spinning through the weeks behind, connecting for her the days, the week. And the mortar, that ornamental bamboo pipe, marking the passing of each moment.

At first she could not stand the mortar, like a loud, clacking clock in the garden, like a self-important mechanical duck, its bamboo throat filling with water, then clapping down empty spilling water upon the stones. Again and again. It did not disturb Jun, beside her he slept, she watched him most nights in the moonlight that speared a crack in the window shutters. Clack, clack.

Through the frozen nights, through the icicles that formed like daggers in the pond about the water plants. Through the frost that made of moss between small trees hard, bruised passages of ground. She had never been so cold. There seemed in the house a blatant disregard for the necessity of creature comforts. Or they simply did not feel it. Her mother-in-law was wrapped snugly into layer upon layer of winter kimono, bound at the midriff, tight and firm, and Aunt Fumi sagged untidily beneath muddy-coloured woollens, thick stockings and thicker underwear. They sat mostly beside a few smouldering bits of charcoal in a green china brazier. Sometimes they lit the oil stove, but opened a chink in the window to dissipate the fumes. The cold was at her fingertips in the touch of frozen glass, the wood upon the bannisters, the dark corners in the upper storey of the house. Hirata-*san*, the ancient maid, survivor of another era, gold-toothed and spry as morning light, delighted in a pocket warmer and electric slippers plugged in at the sink. Green lichen on stone lanterns froze, cold tiles near the bath tub made her feet ache. The blooms on a bush of white camellia, small and pinched, soon died and faded to the colour of brown paper. Pipes burst. A frozen kitten was found dead at the gate. Then there was snow, its white light illuminating the secrets of the house and its fossilised interiors. She cried with the frugality, discomfort and cold.

'So soon?' Jun had said. 'Just because of a little cold?' And from an iron-bound chest pulled out two padded men's kimono, slipped them one inside the other and held it open for her. It barely met across her distended belly. She looked down forlornly as he laughed, turning her around and around, winding the thin silk *obi* low beneath her stomach as if she were a man.

'This is the coldest part of the winter. We call it *daikan*.' And he had shown her a photograph in the newspaper of half-naked kindergarten children exercising in the snow. 'We breed hardiness early. We learn to live with nature, we do not kick against it. We don't cosset ourselves with central heating, electric blankets and the like,' he had laughed.

'Why not? Why not? Why suffer like this?'

'We do not feel it as you do. You too will learn,' he promised.

Even her thoughts had frozen.

But the next day he came home with an electric blanket, with thick, sock slippers and a mohair shawl. Then she had felt better, the bed was warm. She was a hibernating thing in a secret nest unsavaged by the season. She resisted when they came to roll the quilts away, to face her again with bare floors. She begged she was unwell, that she needed to rest through the day.

'It is not customary,' said Itsuko when she heard, tight-lipped, 'for quilts to be left like that all day. It is a sign of slovenliness. They must be folded and stored, the table and cushions must be laid out instead.'

But Kate had clung to her bed, swaddled and warm, her brittle emotions thawing, taking on once more vital form. She feigned exhaustion, which was not untrue. But after two days Fumi swirled in again with the maid, opening windows, whipping up quilts, spilling them out upon the thick tiled roof to air. The room was filled by a frozen gust, and the precious yellow rectangle of her electric blanket was shaken free of the bed. Fumi laughed and laughed, soft and kind, and soon brought an extra oil stove, dusty still with cobwebs, from a forgotten cubby-hole.

Unable to sleep, Kate got up again and went to the window, to watch for Jun's return. A single clear pane of glass had been fitted into the frosted window, for she had found it unbearable, not to see out. She spent a great part of each day in the room, and the opaque window threw her in upon herself, cutting her off from the world outside, refusing to reveal sharp mornings or the passage of the day upon the sun. To observe these things she must open the window and meet an Arctic blast. It became a point of desperation that she herself did not understand. If she could see the sky, the road, the tops of trees, something in her might be eased.

'But it is precisely because you should *not* see the road, and not be *seen* from it. It is for privacy,' Itsuko explained stiffly, unable to understand such a blatant need to display oneself to the curiosity of the world. She was adamant on the matter, but gave way at last to Jun's persuasion. Kate stood before the window now in the dark, staring out, waiting for Jun to return. The waterfall rushed on behind her thoughts.

A few flakes of snow drifted down, then quickened in a sudden flurry and stopped again. In the distance she could see the lights of the town and beyond it the bay, its vast black waste of water illuminated by the moon that rose above the small stout trees of the garden. The branches of an old loquat tree clawed against the glass in a breeze, and the bamboo mortar continued to knock unceasingly on the stones beside the pond, almost hidden by a dwarfed and ancient fir. There was nothing to be seen of the waterfall. It lay at the back, beyond the compound of the house, fed by springs and streams spilling down from the pine covered hills that backed the town of Kobe.

Nothing was anything like Kate had imagined.

2

What right had she, what right? Jun stared at his mother, standing beside him. This factory at least had been his own to manage as he wished; she had not visited it regularly. Itsuko's perfume among the heavy smells of machinery was something thin and slippery. He swallowed angrily. Before him in the factory, within the new machine, thread spun faster and faster, twisted upon small pockets of air, invisibly pressured and manipulated. He waited knowing what would happen. The thread snapped, the machine slowed and stopped. 'It's too soon, I told you,' Jun said. 'There are adjustments to be made.'

'Again. Try again.' Itsuko took no notice of him, commanding the foreman.

Anger knotted in Jun. The man looked at him in query, and he nodded reluctantly. The machine was started, the thread snapped again.

'It's not good enough, not running at the speed you promised,' Itsuko admonished.

'It will,' Jun replied as calmly as he could. 'We still need time. These things are not achieved overnight.'

'Work faster then. Tamura has begun work on a similar device. We must patent this before he progresses any further.' Itsuko ordered.

'Tamura can do nothing. As I heard he has already abandoned the project. He hasn't a work team like ours.'

'Still, we can't risk being beaten by that upstart,' Itsuko stated.

'Just wait a little longer,' Jun insisted. His mother had invested money and her pride in this invention, but he had invested emotion, as had everybody standing tensely about the machine.

He had warned her not to test it now. He bit his tongue, swallowing words that came to his lips. What right had she, the machine was *his* idea, *his* conviction. While he had been away she did not care if it failed, but now she sensed success she was anxious to control. It would be another achievement in her name; to spin at twice the speed of conventional machines, taking crude thread to its final stage in an arrogant rejection of orthodoxy; all she wanted was that glory.

He watched her turn and leave, and after a moment followed her out as she made her way to another shed on her inspection of the plant. The morning sunlight was thin and sharp and glittered on the metal of cars in front of the office. Tiny and frail, his mother walked ahead through the blending and the carding sheds, never overpowered by the group of men about her. Itsuko's will turned the balance of equations upside down. Even from a distance Jun felt the hard, fierce light within her.

The high-roofed sheds, their roof beams dusty with fluff, were filled with machines, row upon row, snapping and moving in unison. Itsuko surveyed them like an army as they clicked and purred. The air that was thick and moist from wheezing vaporisers. Jun stepped back before a large vacuum cleaner patrolling a row of machines, sucking up dust. Combed thread ran in waterfalls over the rollers before him; he felt as if the machines communicated to him. He could not help his bitterness. All this before him was supposedly his, but how long before he could claim it? His mother should have retired as expected several years before, and more and more he found he resented her manipulation and control. Each way he turned she confronted him, depriving him of an independence that would have made his life worthwhile; she allowed him no ultimate responsibility. He had not felt this way before he went abroad. His three years away, accountable only to himself, had been an education not easily relinquished, but his mother blamed this sudden restlessness on his unsuitable marriage. Since then she delighted in extracting the most from the dark space that now existed between them. He knew it was his punishment.

Throughout his life her expectations had followed him. 'You are a Nagai. People's eyes are upon you and what account you give of yourself to the world.' He remembered her expression as she spoke, colourless as glass behind her words. He remembered hearing them once on the edge of a moonlit garden as she chastised him for some prank. As she spoke the moon withdrew behind a band of clouds. Cold, defeated and nine years old, he had stared at her in contrition. She had waited for his apology, and as he spoke the moon reappeared in the sky. *You are a Nagai.* Responsibility settled upon his tiny frame and dissolved within his mind. He never forgot, except when he married Kate.

Kate. In the beginning it had seemed so simple. He wanted her. He was used to having the women he wanted but with Kate the affair did not end with that slowing to boredom in himself as it did with other women. Instead, the need for her thickened in him, spreading, pushing into every corner of his mind and body. The light on leaves and the sharp shadows between tall buildings were like the thought of her. Each day seemed thin without her, until he was frightened. Until then love had been to him a matter safely confined; romance was the simple illusion of women's magazines. He was unprepared for the sudden widening of horizon, the discovery of a new level of deep feeling. It was a revelation to him.

Until he met Kate he had also felt in London as if fallen from another planet, with senses and feelings of no use in that world. He knew Kate was impressed by his knowledge of Western culture, of music, art and history. But these things were just the embroidery on a cushion of knowledge available to any educated Japanese. The stuffing inside was another matter, as impenetrable an enigma as his own culture was to Kate.

In Japan all inner thoughts and self were guarded from the world, every daily meeting meticulously dictated in word and action the distance between men. The careless familiarity he found abroad unsettled him until he learned through Kate that this spontaneity was not always what it seemed. Through her he perceived a deliberate structure in a culture he had found difficult to understand before. He began to absorb an ideology that contradicted all he knew. Kate took him into a new dimension. When the thought of marriage first came to him he pushed it aside. The image of his mother polarised his thoughts, not only did he contemplate a marriage of his choice, but to a foreigner whom his society would not easily accept.

There was another shadow too, that lay in his mind like a still, dark pool. How he wondered could he live with *that*? What would Kate do if she ever knew? He pushed the thought away. It would remain what it was, a secret, just a shadow in his mind.

When he returned he would deal with it. There were ways. If he was careful Kate need never know. He had pushed the tangles from his mind, allowed himself the licence of impulse and spontaneity, the new doctrine he had learned. He had asked Kate to marry him.

That distant time in London appeared far away now, as he watched the combing machines spin around. His mother called to him from where she stood beside another machine, her small, bright eyes questioning him.

After the inspection there was a quick lunch of eel and rice. They ate in the upstairs conference room they used at the plant, when they came out twice a week from the Osaka office. Jun finished his meal and took in his hands the small bowl of tea. He had lost count of the times he had eaten in this room, the times he had sat in this same chair. Every piece of furniture had been in this room as far back as he could remember. As a small child he had sometimes accompanied his father to the factory and sat here, in this room, swinging his legs. Then, as now, they had eaten eel. Then, as now, the huge oil painting on the wall before him had filled him with depression. It had been acquired by his grandfather soon after the Sino-Russian war, the work of a famous Western-style artist. Jun stared at the bleak vastness of war torn Manchuria and the bleaker sight of men and guns, depicted against a stormy sky. The room was clinical in its cold, white hush. Each chair and sofa, crowded one beside the other, was shrouded tightly in white covers and antimacassars, a white cloth draped the large table beneath a sheet of clear plastic. There were the same bare worn boards beneath his feet that still echoed and creaked. Nothing had changed. Everything was as he remembered.

Beyond the room there was always the loud din of movement. When he came to the factory as a child with his father he remembered there were always new machines, each more dazzling than the last, rattling and racing miles of yarn faster and thinner year by year. There were always new buildings and facilities in progress. Now there were things *he* wanted to see implemented here, things *he* wanted to do. All that time in England his mind had been alert to every scrap of information that might be of use in the expansion of Nagai. He had notebooks full of points of relevance he had wished later to apply. But since his return to Japan he could not place these new perspectives anywhere. Frustration throbbed within him, the hushed white certainty of this one, unchanging room closed about him. As nothing had changed within it over the years, so it seemed nothing could change within him.

Later, there was a meeting with some of the staff. Jun sat beside his chief manager at the plant, Yamamura, who coughed, chestily, as he sat down at the conference table. A plump flaccid figure in his beige overalls, everything about him was soft and malleable except his shifty eyes. Jun regarded him wearily; whatever his performance, they could never get rid of Yamamura. He was a cousin of Itsuko's and had been promoted on Jun's father's death to the headship of the business by a family council. Itsuko at once assured her joint control by stepping in for Jun, the child heir. She soon learned to undermine Yamamura's territory and consolidate her own. Inclined to *mahjong*, women and the bars, he entered with Itsuko's encouragement a new phase of self-indulgence, relieved to relinquish the complexities of command to her able mind. He made no effort to obstruct Itsuko's rise to power, the balance in their partnership was of satisfaction to them both. Beside Jun at the table, he picked a tooth and explained to Itsuko the proposals of the labour unions for the annual Spring offensive.

With the absence of any powerful national unions, company unions negotiated individually with their separate managements. The labour union leaders sat in an orderly group at the end of the table, waiting their turn to speak. Jun listened intently to the voices about him, to the quiet presentation of arguments, each like a well-worn actor's role, devoid of heat or whittled edge. They went through this regularly twice a year, the results always the same small, inflexible advance by the unions. It was all quite different from his observations abroad and he was thankful for this native, orderly system of things. But that time abroad had changed him. On his return he found himself agreeing with a small radical group of businessmen who were voicing a need for modifications to cope with a complex future. Attitudes everywhere were changing, there were advances to make for a final break with feudalism into full maturity. He had recently written an article for a business magazine in which he had stated that the British factory had the complexity of a jungle, full of dark corners no one dared touch for fear of finding a viper's nest, and that the Japanese factory had the aseptic fixed complexity of an overplanned maze. His mother, when he repeated this, had refused to see any change must come. They argued endlessly, Itsuko always adamant that the traditions that served so well in the past and produced their present prosperity were valid for the future. Because of his views she held back even more, he suspected, on the responsibility he craved. If she could not retire she should have the grace to recede to another role and place, supportive yet behind him. How long must he wait, he wondered again?

They were now discussing with a group of senior managers the addition of an extra verse to the factory song. There had been a competition amongst the workers to submit the new verse; a verse to the true spirit of harmony. The winner stood up and smoothed his hair and cleared his throat before them.

May the plans we make today
Be the promise of tomorrow.
May our spirits lead us on
Towards the high ideals of our
Ultimate achievement.
For the honour of Nagai.

Behind Jun the workers' delegation clapped, joined by the labour leaders. Itsuko smiled and nodded, looking towards Jun. He stood up to make the acceptance speech. His mother watched him as he spoke, her eyes bright, but he was aware of a critical element in her gaze that he had never felt before. Although there was no way to overcome her disappointment in his marriage, there was not now that daily crucifixion. They had moved, he and Kate, into a home of their own. It was temporary, for he wanted to buy land and build. It was far from ideal, only two blocks from Itsuko and one of several properties she owned. But they were alone, no longer subjected to her vigilant inspection. He had it in mind to move since Itsuko told him the tenant was relocating to Tokyo. He had approached his mother the night Kate had been so upset, the night of their wedding anniversary.

'It will be better,' he had said to Itsuko, 'if you have not to see her before you all the time. Better for us all.'. He sat alone with her and Fumi.

'What difference does that make to my disappointment?' Itsuko's insisted, tight and hard. He had never apologised for his marriage.

'I am thinking only of you. For Kate, in her present condition, it will not be easy to cope with a household. I am anxious for you and the strain upon your nerves. There will at least be peace, if we move. It is only two blocks, far enough to ease the strain, yet near enough for contact between you and I.'

He feared she would not agree. Age had not softened her beyond a slight slackening of the skin. She saw things only as shapes to be moulded in her hands. In the darkness of the room the low lamp had picked out the outline of her nostril and the thick double fold of her lids.

Kate, Fumi told them, had gone to bed, exhausted by distress. He had thought of Kate in the room above, thought of the coldness with which he was forced to treat her before his mother. She did not understand the inequalities that were here the rule of life, and dictated a differing patterning of affection. Her faith in freedom and equality, her spontaneous response to everything were poles apart from the world he lived in, where each was allotted a proper station, rigid in its order and nature of response. In the room above she waited, weary of this constant, vicious game. Across the table Fumi sat crocheting, her little hook moved deftly to the mortar's constant clack, clack, clack in the garden.

'Perhaps you are right. Perhaps it is better that you move. We shall tell people your wife could not adapt to our Japanese ways. People will understand,' Itsuko acquiesced, inclining her head with a gracious nod.

Too easy, too soft. So that immediately he had wondered what she was scheming. And at the same time thought, it did not matter. They would be alone, they would have some life she could not touch.

'We are moving,' he had whispered into Kate's ear. 'We will be alone in a home of our own.' She came into his arms then, and the tenderness between them that night lasted like a secret.

From the next morning Kate had been different, calmer, brighter, hope was a weakness she could not hide. Alone at last in their small, bare home the hard shapes that had encased them for weeks dissolved. They were like children released from school, brimming. With a young maid Kate worked through each day until the house was flushed with the crisp, sharp smell of scrubbing, of dark corners released to sun. Everywhere, there was the slosh of cloths and bucket upon bucket of water. Suddenly in the rooms there was the clean, bright movement of cushions and curtains and plants and flowers. Armfuls of flowers stuck thick and tall into wide-necked vases.

'Not those poor solitary blooms manipulated to rigid rules, not a petal out of place. I want free and messy vases.' Kate laughed. They had both forgotten she could laugh.

'Happy?' he asked. 'Happy now?' and was glad for her, wishing to give her the world then. Loving her.

Now, in the conference room, the factory clock ticked away the afternoon, moving with arthritic clicks. Outside, the roof of the blending shed was like the dark back of an animal. The labour union leaders stood up and in an orderly crocodile, filed from the room. It was nearly time to go. Jun stacked up his papers and excused himself from the room. He could not use the phone there, nor the one in the office downstairs. He went instead to the public phone before the workers' canteen. The area was deserted, it was not an hour for meals. He dialled the number quickly, and listened to the ring. The child answered in its piping, baby voice.

'Your mother. Call your mother,' he said. And almost immediately he heard her voice.

'Chieko?' he said. 'I'll come this evening, but not for long.'

'As always, I'll be waiting,' she replied.

He replaced the phone and turned away. The thought of Kate fragmented him. But what could he do? There was no choice. He turned back towards the building. In the lighted window of the second storey he saw his mother descending the stairs.

3

There were times now in the mornings when bare trees were festooned with flocks of tiny warblers, pale as old grey moss. They quarrelled in the willow tree and the swelling branches of the cherry. They would only sing, Aunt Fumi said, when the blossoms burst and bloomed. The sun was yellow and firm, about the sudden fragrance of a flowering bush, and lay light and lemon coloured on the stones beyond the porch. Kate took her breakfast into the garden. Her companion at these times was often a book of Japanese grammar. She felt better now she was more fluent in the language. She believed she was beginning to speak with a natural ear. The lack of communication was the worst thing that faced any new arrival. Kate was thankful for her ability to learn a language quickly.

On a chair in the porch she drowsed and drifted when not reading, the short morning's warmth was soft on the skin, precious as the solitude she could now enjoy. The house was her own, its rooms free of other people's thoughts and the dark accumulation of emotion. She felt the need to wander through them several times a day, looking and planning. She had already divided the rooms, new furniture was ordered and arriving every day. Fresh paint filled the house with light. It was all decided, each corner and accessory. Her mind and body ached with the shopping and anticipation, but it was nearly finished, and slowly there grew around her a world of her own choosing; an upright world of sideboards and tables and familiar perspectives. In the drape of chintz, the shine of wax, she thought she found a relevance that had thwarted her until now.

For the child there was a small, white room opening off their own. There was a chest with nursery characters and a lamp shaped like a bunch of balloons. Her emotions overflowed at the thought of the small and milky presence that would inherit all these things. Already, the drawers in the room were full of tiny knitted garments, but it was still difficult to relate these things to the child that stirred inside her.

She rarely saw Itsuko; a silent, mutual understanding agreed upon by everyone concerned. From a window of the bedroom Kate could see the corner of a roof of the main house some distance down the hill. And the waterfall connected them, for the stream, like a moving thread cut down beside both homes. Its sound rushed through each day and each night, knotting her present life to its recent past. She saw Fumi every day, visiting or visited. Their relationship was easy and comforting to Kate, and sometimes conspiratorial. In her loose, overstretched woollens, Fumi sat with her back to the sun in the newly painted lounge, and the light was soft and yellow, filling her lap. She lowered her voice to counsel small things. A cake to please Itsuko, the use of wheat tea for drunkenness and a paste of beans for burns. She told of the superhuman power of foxes and the danger of possession and how their evil spirits entered through the space between flesh and fingernails. She advised on brands of vinegar and soap and counselled the importance of directions; the east was luckiest, northeast the devil's door. She was horrified to find they innocently slept with their heads due north, in which direction corpses were laid, and demanded immediate rearrangement. The bright vanity of Kate's rooms was a marvel to Fumi. She touched the chintz and the velvet cushions and the baskets for bread in gentle, curious pleasure, but drew back at the brink of this alien world, preferring the cluttered frugality of her own. She hurried back guiltily to the sunless rooms of the family house and her sister's evening meal.

Sometimes, when she knew Itsuko was out, Kate returned to the main house to visit Fumi. The old house had a sad solemnity that both compelled and repelled her. She liked to sit with Fumi in her room, their feet beneath the quilt that skirted the *kotatsu*, the table topped foot-warmer. On this quilt were printed the clouds and birds and wild plants of some secret garden world. Fumi's room looked out at the back of the house onto a murmuring pine and the leaves of an elderberry. The light shifted and fell through the boughs, dull and green as old bronze, to lift the shadows of the room. It seemed to Kate the room held the very shape of Fumi's life. There was a touch of dampness and the smell of old paper. Tall, worn chests, grain shiny with age, contained in their dark recesses the punctuation of a life. Fumi lifted out gently the burnished folds of her wedding kimono and spilt them across the floor, rich and soft as the thoughts that had once briefly filled her. She displayed with a laugh the white hood worn by brides to cover their 'devil's horns.' For a moment a tiny, appliquéd apron brought back to life a daughter. A spotted yellow square of newspaper froze forever in its mildewed type the graduation of a son. Two small wooden boxes, ribbon bound, revealed shrivelled leather worms that were the umbilical cords of these forgotten babies. The picture of a thick-jowled husband, a silver thimble, a temple charm, a pressed spring flower; the smell of mothballs bound together the memories in that cold, green lighted world. And in the kitchen, dark and brown as the rest of the house, old Hirata-*san* washed rice in a tiled sink. Here Fumi explained the preparation of a pickle bed that could last for generations. She revealed the mysterious properties of soybean paste and the *ying* and *yang* of vegetables. She insisted that a bowl of Japanese soup with its fermented enzymes and sea mosses, was a condensed form of the ancient, primordial sea. She demonstrated the art of cutting that could turn a common stump of turnip into a chrysanthemum. She was a land, she was a culture, she was a history in herself. But more than this she was comfort and love.

So that, when Kate returned to her own home, she was enlightened and enriched, but sometimes confused. She walked back up the winding road to her own small home, her mind still full of the old house with its faint smell of drains, and creaking corridors. And the strange details Fumi always imparted remained embedded in her mind, like rare stones in an old jewel box. As she opened her gate she looked up at the firred slopes of Mount Rokko from the garden of her home, and wondered at her presence in this densely detailed and unfamiliar world. Then, for a while, it seemed as if the shadowy residue of the main house had followed her, and filled her own home. But the feeling faded, her rooms returned to the familiar essence she demanded about her. She sighed and noted the passing of yet another day.

But there were other confusions, less easily dealt with. When they first moved into their own house, they had been like children, released from the imprisonment of their own bodies.

Each day they arranged their furniture and promptly rearranged it, laughing and unravelling potential future worlds. It all seemed as full as full; until Jun did not return on time, once or twice, then frequently, detained on the way home by Itsuko at the old house, on one pretext or another. He phoned and his voice was concise, as if his mother's eyes encased him. He must stay, he said, for dinner, there was business to discuss. When he returned he could only explain, there was nothing he could do. It was not a question of personal preference, but a matter of order and obligation. It was not possible in his circumstances to elevate a wife above a mother.

She tried to understand. To greet him cheerfully when he returned and ease the strain she saw in his face, at the divisions apparent in him. It was not his fault, it was an order of life that would have raised few questions in a Japanese woman. For this reason Kate tried to grasp the restrictions of her role and contain the bitterness growing within her. But there were other evenings when he did not return, that she remembered noting even when they lived in the old house. But then, preoccupied with the difficulties of life with Itsuko, she had not noticed each new detail of Jun's daily routine. Now she found there were evenings when the obligations of work forced him into a ribald world, the thought of which unexpectedly enraged her. This was a side of Japan she had been unprepared for among the exotics and aesthetics, a neon-lighted dissolute world of bars, of women and drink, that seemed to play such a part in everyday life and was essential, it seemed, for business.

'It is the custom, I cannot refuse to go, I cannot escape even if I wished to. Business associates expect it of me. Here it is difficult sometimes to know where business ends and leisure begins. You must understand. It is only a drink, nothing more,' Jun told her firmly. But beside him in bed, while he slept heavily and the smell of drink escaped from him, she was filled by a fury she did not understand. She closed her eyes and tried to ignore the scent of that other dissolute world that so frequently claimed him, beyond the life they lived together. She would learn, she supposed. She trusted him.

For one reason or another then, there were many evenings spent alone. Jun returned always apologetic and tender, and she tried to assure him she did not mind. She believed she was learning to accept a different and difficult order of things. There was also the pleasure of the growing comfort of the house, and the child, turning within her, evolving for her the sureness of a future. And she was also filled with new confidence, for Paula and Pete had returned to Japan, reassigned again to Kobe. It made all the difference to know she had a friend.

It was strange to see Paula, settled on a hill above Kitano-cho in a draughty house that was in style neither Japanese nor Western. It was strange to see emerge from the pile of crates scattered throughout the house, the familiar objects she had seen before in their London home. The repatriated bric-a-brac, re-rooted now in its original soil, appeared self-consciously decorative. Looking once more at the woodblock prints of sumo wrestlers on the wall, at the candlestick lamp and the lacquer bowls, Kate felt she retraced herself in time. She stared again at the *kai-oki* box and remembered the night Jun explained it at that party long ago. Suddenly everything about her was familiar and known. There was James, the Baileys' son, scattering his war planes about the house, there was Paula's embroidery frame flung untidily onto a cushion. There was the toss and banter of words between Pete and Paula, in a way she had forgotten. With the Baileys' return a whole stiff, traumatised section of herself struggled back to life. She may have changed, thought Kate, but nothing changed the Baileys, they retained their identity anywhere in the world. She remembered again then the Baileys' pale, bare rooms in Pimlico above an antique shop. She remembered a threadbare tapestry behind a lacquered Chinese chest in the window of the shop. And she remembered the afternoon, so long ago now, when upstairs in Paula's flat the sun had set in a pallid winter sky and she had told Paula that Jun had asked her to marry him. She did not know why she recalled that sky, except that it seemed the future began that afternoon. She remembered the Baileys' words of caution, and their advice about Japan. There was nothing she could change, nor would if it were possible.

She put a hand upon her belly then, possessive of the future, and realised that the child had not stirred for several days.

4

She heard the door close and then the room was silent and dark. Where would they take the child now? The thought was a pain no one could stop. The dusk, like an ugly spreading bruise, covered the walls, thickening in corners. The clank of the trolley pushed by the nurses faded from the corridor, now the loud caw of a crow outside carved suddenly into the evening. Her hands stretched on the strange flat expanse of her belly, then lay still again upon the white covers of the narrow hospital bed.

She had held the child in her arms and felt its tiny weight. She had touched with a finger the black spikes of fine hair, the little creases and folds of its face. And only then had she seen the stillness and heard the silence of those before her. Only then had she seen the child was dead.

'A beautiful baby, a boy.' The nurse bent to touch Kate's arm. 'Stillborn ... I'm sorry ... there was nothing ...' She heard the sympathy in their voices like sounds from another world. She had clung to the child then, to that still, small weight, like a nugget of hope in her arms. But they handled her firmly, they handled her calmly. Now they were gone, the room was dark, the crow rasped once again. Before her was space and yet more space, as void as her emptied body.

'Kate, Kate.' The sound pulled her forward, and she opened her eyes. Above her she saw the face of her husband and hated him for the first time in their brief married life. Seeing Jun she saw again the child and the same set of their eyes. Go away. The words welled up but lay mute on her tongue. Then she closed her eyes again and was ashamed, for there was nothing he had done.

Soon she was back in the ward, the room was warm with the glow of a lamp. In a corner Aunt Fumi's comfortable shadow scratched her head with a crochet hook, then continued to structure a doily. She sighed unfolding cotton skeins, head bent again to her work.

'Kate.' His voice was near her ear this time, he sat on a chair by the bed.

'Did they show him to you?' Jun took Kate's hand, the silence shapeless between them.

'I saw him,' she whispered.

Kate heard Fumi sigh, a small, sad sound like the shutting of a book. Where had they taken the baby? Wherever they had they put him it could be nowhere near the other babies. The pain returned then faded, Kate closed her eyes and slept.

Jun waited, but Kate did not stir, in sleep her face was peaceful. He stood up slowly then, and made his way to the telephone in the lobby, for he could delay the call to Itsuko no longer. His mother had just returned home, Hirata-*san* announced. Itsuko's voice was as always, cool and divorced of emotion. But he knew she was waiting, he had heard the slight edge, like the arc of a blade in her voice. Without elaboration he told her what he had to.

'A stillbirth ... ?' She repeated his words and he heard strength return to her voice, until it rang with relief.

'It's too late now, I shall come in the morning. Fumi will stay this first night. You must go home and rest.' Her voice was soft with sudden warmth. Before the telephone Jun gave a small bow of respect before he replaced the receiver.

She came as promised in the morning, to the private maternity home, the chauffeur walking behind her with a massive basket of fruit. The shroud of mauve cellophane wrapping crackled and turned the yellow of grapefruit and apples to a sickly undertone, a red ribbon sealed the package. Stood upon a table, the basket appeared to Kate half as big as her mother-in-law.

As soon as she entered, Itsuko possessed the room, it condensed about her so that nothing else was of importance. She pulled a chair up to Kate's bed.

'So sad, such a pity. I'm filled with sympathy for you.' Her face arranged regret, but her voice remained compact beneath a slight inflection. She smoothed the kimono over her knee and her hands lay calm and white as two fans upon her lap.

In her corner Fumi continued to crochet, but glanced out of her flat and plain brown face at the immaculate back of her elder sister. Stuffed down deep in a linen knitting bag, unfinished baby clothes lay in the chair beside her.

'She slept well, but ate only a little breakfast, just a bowl of *miso* soup.'

'Now that will not do. You must eat and regain your strength. An apple would do you good. I shall peel you one myself.' Itsuko fussed.

Taking a plate and a knife from Fumi, she lifted the crackling mauve cellophane and retrieved a giant apple. Spreading a handkerchief on her knee she placed the plate on it and began to peel the fruit. Soon apple skin grew in an unbroken waxy rope from her polished fingers.

'Here you are. Let me see you eat.' Itsuko offered the cut fruit to Kate.

It was as if some rite had been performed. She refolded the handkerchief on her knee, then drew from her handbag a tissue to dab her fingers. This too was then neatly folded and laid in an ashtray. Her movements were like the gestures of some rarely seen performance. Kate could not remember in the few months she had known her mother-in-law, a show of such concern. At the wash basin Itsuko rinsed the apple juice from her hands. Fumi rested her crochet hook in a thicket of lace and stared warily at her sister's back, and then back at Kate.

They waited for her in the office, an important conference had been arranged, Jun may already be there. Itsuko threw the words lightly about, patting her hair before the mirror. Kate did not trust herself to speak, for she knew why an undisguisable glitter illuminated Itsuko this morning. But soon she was gone, no more than footsteps fading down the corridor, accompanied by Fumi to her car. For some time after her departure, the empty room remained shaped by her perfume, a dark, uneasy smell. She would not visit again, and she was glad, Kate knew, that the child was dead. She had not wanted a half-caste grandchild, to sully the Nagai dynasty.

She heard the door opening and Fumi's return. Her kindly presence was beside Kate again. It was a reassuring custom that allowed a relative some share of nursing duties. Fumi insisted she stay at the nursing home with Kate, and Itsuko agreed, and also arranged a private nurse to supplement hospital staff. Kate clung to Fumi, whose flat face gave comfort.

'Don't let her upset you, you'll bleed the more.' Fumi spoke quietly, touching Kate's face with a cool, damp cloth. A faint smell of cologne drifted from her, like perfume left in an empty drawer. Her skin was soft and pouched on the unadorned planes of her face, and like her sister her hair was kept resolutely black, but in a short hard perm. Sad memories slipped from her in the gentle touch of her hands.

'There will be other times, other babies.' She plumped up a pillow and replaced it beneath Kate's head. 'You must put this behind you.'

She sat back on her chair, absorbed in her crocheting again, the growing blond doily trembling gently in her hands. To Kate's sleepy eyes the tangle of cotton seemed to grow, expanding to fill the room like a thick skeined web above her bed. And hanging from the centre, staring down out of a bleached and knotted halo, Kate imagined the face of her mother-in-law, eyes infused with malice.

Through the window the sun was warm on her arm, and the cobalt tiles of a neighbouring roof blazed molten in the morning. A fly settled on a water jug and proceeded to clean its wings. She observed these things, yet none seemed as real as the great basket of fruit, moored near the bed, like a ship with a cellophane sails. The empty paper nest that had held the giant apple stared out like a missing eye. She wanted to scream, but the moment passed, and her eyes filled with tears at last. Beside her, Fumi and her little hook knitted a tangled world. On the windowsill Kate counted the bodies of dead flies.

She reached out and from the bedside cabinet took up the letter she had received that morning from her mother.

'Dear Katherine.' Opening it again she read once more the bright, chatty lines littered with inflated details and holding in their school blue ink her mother's personality and a distant world. And reading, that world filled Kate's again like a forgotten dream. None of it seemed part of her, none of it seemed real. She remembered the day she had first taken Jun to meet her mother, and indicated their future plans. Mrs Scott had been agreeable, sitting in her flat facing Putney Heath, surrounded by her memories of a travelled life in India before Kate was born, late and nearly not at all. Mrs Scott, widowed, plump, full of causes, committees and borrowed opinions, slim at the ankle, full at the hip; Mrs Scott did not object.

'The world,' said Mrs Scott, sitting between many occasional tables, a fat tabby cat on her lap, 'The world nowadays is a very small place. And I have always been so fascinated by the beautiful works of Utamaru. Such a highly decorative art, and yet not decorative as we translate it, which is the light result of mere copying. Oh no. One lump or two, dear?' pouring tea into translucent cups. 'And not to forget Pussums,' as the cat stretched impatiently on her lap, kneading its claws, starting a ladder in the stockings under her heather tweed skirt. She placed a saucer on the floor and reached low with the milk jug to fill it. The cat jumped down and began to lick before the stream was finished.

'Katherine is an adaptable girl. I'm sure she will make an easy transition to living in Japan. What an interesting country, so picturesque and exotic. How I envy you both.' Mrs Scott handed a cup to Jun. 'A wholemeal scone dear, or a scotch pancake? Her father and I lived, you know, many years in India. I adapted, I found and took the best. It's a question of mind, and also of spirit.' Mrs Scott recalled again the lawns of the club in Delhi, spread with tables and basket chairs, the turbaned waiters the only colour in her all-white world. The bridge tables in the card rooms, the lazy turning fans, and the sunburned necks of Englishmen as they clustered in the bar. She remembered the taste of daiquiris and the smell of jasmine in the evening. The rest she refused to recall. But she had no doubt she had adapted. Had she not survived and returned?

'Now tell me about that old man Hokusai who lived to such a grand old age and could even they say, paint with his toes.' Katherine tells me, dear, that you come from a very old line, from the old aristocracy. We too trace ourselves back a long way. I'll show you our little treasures.' She had unlocked the small glass box on the mantelpiece and brought back in her hands the bits and pieces. 'This locket was given to one of our ancestors by Elizabeth the First. It should be in a museum. And the ring and the silver doublet button, see.' She sat down again beside Jun. Kate remembered how impressed he seemed.

'We are an old family, but we were always merchants, we had to marry into Samurai class,' he told Kate afterwards, as if confessing something.

She remembered too how she had sat back, relieved at their collusion over the past, and turned to look at the photograph of her father on the mantelpiece. He stood, stiff and proud beside Mountbatten, before the open door of an ancient car in India. She remembered him always patient with her mother. He sat quietly with his pipe and heard her out on everything. He knew how to handle her, which was more than Kate could do. His death had been devastating to Kate. It had surprised her to see how quickly her mother rose to the organisation of a new life. Within a year Kate went to University to read modern languages and did not come home again. Her mother, when she saw her, was filled with work for Oxfam, societies and committees for saving old buildings; she had covered her sense of loss. For Kate it continued, for years she heard the knock of her father's pipe and his sane advice on her fears.

She had looked away from the photograph to her mother and Jun, wishing it was her father who sat there. But strangely, although it seemed impossible in Jun's broad oriental features and short, sturdy frame to find any likeness to her father, there seemed in his manner a quiet strength she found familiar.

In the beginning, she remembered now, it had been all learning with Jun, every day a new facet or clue to fit to the jigsaw of him. She learned of his kindness and humour, his attention to details in manner and dress, his eye for the shape and the colour of a thing. She learned of tolerances, and intolerances that sometimes surprised her. Each small learning appeared a destination in a strange voyage of discovery. But sometimes when she surfaced from the journey of love, in dark night hours between the dreams, it seemed it was herself she was discovering, and that of him, in spite of all she had learned, she knew not the slightest thing. Then his face rose before her in the night, his smile hiding in its depth the very secret of himself, some mysterious point deep within him that never would be shared. There were things she felt he shut off in himself in closed boxes, like the strange black lacquer cases of esoteric images she had read were kept in Japanese temples that were opened sometimes, or sometimes never touched. And in spite of the love between them, she felt within him she had her own small box that he opened and closed when he pleased.

Yet she was sure she loved him, whatever that word might mean. But the weighing of it was impeded by the physical feelings he filled her with. What she had taken for a suaveness she soon found was the animality of the sure, hard-muscled cat, naked in his purpose. He was a small, physical man. And she remembered when she let herself, the rather tired, dispassionate way he looked at the women about him: as if at some time he had had them all. But these thoughts only filled her with rich and sinuous feelings, and drew her under, away from clear observation. The physical need of him burned in her veins. Whenever they lay together it was never enough. She knew she would follow him anywhere, that all will was completely lost. Now, as she gazed at Fumi intent on her crocheting, these memories seemed so far away in both time and in experience. Now, the jaunty flow of her mother's writing and the bright shapes that they conveyed had little meaning for her.

'Dear Katherine,' she read again. The tears would not stay back then, but ran from her cheeks onto the pillow. Tears for the child and tears for everything else she had lost. The confidence that filled her on arrival and that she struggled so hard to retain was gone. She knew now she faced a future unforeseen in all her dreams. And the thought welled up painfully in her again. Where had they taken the baby? What would they do with him now?

5

The child was still up, he could hear its small, angry cries from behind the door. Chieko was inept at motherhood and slovenly besides. Jun rang the bell again impatiently. The door opened and as soon as she saw him her face became sullen. The child ran to him and pulled at his trouser legs. He bent and picked the boy up. His nose ran, and Jun took out his own handkerchief to wipe it and then sat down in a chair with the child on his lap. She stood in front of him.

'Where were you? Why didn't you come last week? I can't go on like this.' She crossed her arms before him, determined.

'It was difficult. I was busy.' He shrugged. 'Here.' He took a packet from his pocket and laid it on the table. At once she brightened.

'I don't mean to bother you, but I have my problems, I have my difficulties.' She opened the envelope and counted the money inside.

'Only this?' she asked angrily.

'It's enough. What more do you want?' he replied.

'I can't manage on this. I've all kinds of bills at the moment. Yukio's sick as you can see, and I've that coat to pay for.' She nodded to a fur jacket draped over the back of a chair.

'It's not the time of year for fur,' he retorted.

'It's cheaper out of season.'

'That's your affair. I'm not expected to pay for that. I pay the rent, I maintain the child. The rest is not my responsibility.' He sat up angrily. The child began to cry again at their raised voices.

'Father.' The word was stiff and formal in the boy's small, mouth. It was the first word she had taught him to say. She always knew the right move, always knew how to corner him.

'*Ssh.*' He jiggled Yukio on his knee, then pulled from his pocket the bag of sweets and a cheap plastic toy he had bought on the way.

'That's all you think him worth?' Chieko looked bitterly at the toy.

'Get me a coffee. I'm tired.' He stroked the child's hair. 'Have I come here for this?'

'How does it work? Show me,' Yukio held up the toy, smiling at Jun.

'Here,' he said gently, 'this way. Like that. See?' A small, plastic space module shot out into the room and hit a hanging light. Yukio laughed and clapped his hands.

Chieko turned away and went into the kitchen. Soon she reappeared with the coffee, and he saw her expression had changed. She never wasted time with the futile, but moved on to a more efficient wile. She sat down and stirred his coffee for him.

'You do look tired. Come, drink it while it's hot.' Her voice had dropped to the soft and persuasive, she waited meekly at his side. After some time she took the child to bed, insisting suddenly and brusquely when he cried in disappointment.

'Let him stay. I can't be much longer,' Jun said.

'No. It's late,' Chieko replied, pulling the child from him.

He waited aimlessly in the chair, as if he had lost his way and rested for a moment at some impersonal junction. He gazed about the untidy room. Toys, magazines, heaps of clothes, liquor bottles, glasses, cushions were strewn about him with the haphazard neglect of days. The pink carpet was ugly with stains, a bowl of half-eaten soup and noodles, the remains of Yukio's supper, sat on the table congealed and cold. A satin brassiere and a string of folded paper cranes dangled from a chair. The stale smell of the room had been masked by a synthetic air-freshener, the close, sickly smell of lemons filled the air.

Chieko came back into the room and went straight to a bottle of whiskey on a shelf. He shook his head to her enquiry, but she frowned at him sternly and poured two drinks. He watched her rummage for ice in the refrigerator, through the open kitchen door. She was devilishly attractive to him still. In spite of everything, he could not rid himself of the effect she had upon him; it was the reason she had trapped him. She was slim, but with a rare voluptuousness, her hair was coloured a soft cinnamon, and was smooth as plush. Without make-up her skin had a sallow, unhealthy pallor but seemed only to add to her allure. In a high, clear forehead the brows were plucked to almost nothing above her brazen eyes. She could still open with a look that dark secret part within himself like no other woman could. So that for moments at a time he did not recognise himself. He could look at her and think these thoughts and yet still say he loved his wife; he was two men within one body. He turned his eyes away from her.

She brought him the drink and sat close beside him, running a finger over his ear. Looking at his watch, he saw it was early still. He knew too well each the way she had of achieving her purposes. He wished he could leave, that he had the will. But as always when he felt her hands begin their work upon him these thoughts drifted beyond his reach. He knew he was weak. He thought of Kate, but in his mind her face was expressionless and bore no relevancy to the man within this room. He drained the glass of whiskey and allowed its electric pulse to confuse his mind still further. Then he reached across and pulled the woman roughly to him, wishing suddenly to shake and devour her at the same time. She wound herself artfully about him and soon drew him to that point from which there was never a return.

Afterwards, as always now, he hated himself. He prepared quickly to take his leave, pulling on his clothes, smoothing away before a mirror all trace upon him of the woman. She shrugged sourly at his hurry, leaning on the bathroom door.

'When will you come again?'

'I don't know. Soon.'

'Yukio cries for you.'

'No he doesn't. He doesn't know me more than you've taught him to. It's in his own interests that you don't build up much in his mind. I can never recognise him.'

'A father's a father. You can't deny that.'

He was silent and pulled on his jacket, then walked quickly to the door. Outside once more he started the car and drove away, trying to focus his attention, where would it all end? Why could he no longer take this part of his life for the small pleasure it could offer and leave it at that, as any other man would, as he had before he married Kate? Why did he now feel torn apart? He drew up and stopped the car before the damp side of a temple wall. It had begun to rain, and in the light of a street lamp the old stones of the wall were ancient with secrets. He dropped his head in his hands, filled with self-disgust.

He had met her five years before in a bar. He had sought his pleasure where he could then, unrelentingly. He had money, he was a man, and part of a society unhampered by any sense of Christian sin. He lived with the same indulgences his father had before him, as was expected of a man. For the pleasures of the flesh he had been taught to regard as a wholly permissible part of life, in no way related to any other part of himself. He set Chieko up as his mistress, as was not unusual with a woman of her type or a man in his position. It did not disturb him when his mother talked periodically of marriage, although he found excuses always to put it off, when she showed him the formal, posed photographs of girls eligible for his hand. Such an event would anyway be the marrying of his family to another, a duty he must eventually defer to, it was unlikely there would be love. That was no part of the ideal his mother had in mind. He had seen no reason at that time for Chieko in any way to disturb the tempo of his future. But she grew difficult and perverse as their relationship established, several times he tried to cut it off, but somehow her body always drew him back, like a bad spirit, until she told him about the child.

'What?' he had shouted.

She had stood before him, a cool expression on her face and he knew she had planned it.

'You know I can't marry you.' There was no question of that, a woman of her class. But he knew as the words left his mouth that a child would seal them together forever as surely as any marriage. There was no love, just arithmetic in her. And she thought nothing of the child, or the stigma of illegitimacy. She thought only of herself and the advantage it would bring her.

'Get rid of it,' he told her brusquely, pushing her roughly away, so that she stumbled over a chair.

'It'll cost money.' She looked up, her face brazen and hard.

'Here,' he said the next time he saw her, handing her the envelope. There was more than enough, and she understood.

'I'll go away. You won't see me again,' she said defiantly. There had been silence then, and he had relaxed, and put the moment and its horror behind him. Soon the plan for him to go to England to study textile processes began to materialise and he prepared to leave for the stay there. Chieko became just a shadow in his mind, but he should have known better, should have known nothing with Chieko could have been finished so easily. Three weeks before he left for London she reappeared with the child.

'See,' she said. 'See, your son.' She thrust the small bundle at him. He drew back in horror, his dry mouth devoid of words. Small choked noises began in the knitted package, there appeared signs of some weak struggling. He backed further away, she laughed.

'His name,' she said, 'is Yukio.'

And at once, sealed with a name, the woollen parcel began to heave and roar until its cries filled the dark rococo coffee shop where they sat, that he had entered unsuspectingly only moments before. Yukio. The word became the rhythm of the bawling. It filled his head and in one deft stroke shifted his life forever into a different gear. A small, pink foot appeared from the angry bundle and kicked out and kicked over a coffee cup. The contents spilt across the table towards him. He stood up, stared numbly, and fled.

Next she went to his mother, discreetly, politely, adroit and vulpine, the bundle on her arm.

'You must pay,' Itsuko told him, blanched and white as a naked almond. 'You must pay to keep her quiet. Make sure I never see her again, that I hear no more of this.'

He paid and left as quickly as he could for the broad, clean sweep of England. And there the thought of Chieko became thankfully a dream. Only the monthly bank draft tied him sometimes to reality. He locked the secret deep within him. It was as separate and silent and as sealed to him as the dark, buried square of a grave. It did not disturb the daylight or the smooth running of his life. He almost forgot. He met Kate and the past seemed then to sink still further and condense within him. He told Kate nothing. He could find no words and there seemed no need. Only when he returned to Japan did he realise the past was not something so easily shed.

The child was three now, and called him, father. He had imagined only a future of impersonal bank drafts; he had not wanted to see the child. But at his return the machinery of fate seemed to grate into life. Reality now regained a focus and became hard and clear edged. He did not contact Chieko, but she heard about his marriage and demanded that he see her. She demanded more money and occasional visits for the sake of the child. Otherwise, she said, otherwise...

He had no option but to agree. The thought of Kate ever knowing was more than he could bear. He wondered sometimes now how he could have so impassively deceived her. It had been the fear of losing her, and even then he did not have the courage to see upon her face the destruction of everything they had built. He could not take that from her, or risk that she might leave him.

That first time he saw the child after he returned with Kate, Chieko did nothing, she was docile and compliant. She had the instinct of an animal. She mixed a drink and did not even allow their fingertips to meet upon the glass. The child looked at him, with shy but friendly eyes. He could not see himself within the boy, only the set of Chieko's eyes.

The second time he brought some sweets, and another time a toy. He did this from a guilty sense of duty and not from a wish to establish anything with the child. As he thrust his gifts awkwardly at the small boy, Chieko exclaimed and pushed down the child's head in an obligatory bow. Slowly then Yukio began to greet him with an expectant smile.

Once Jun found the door of the flat ajar and entered, unannounced. The child looked at him then scrambled up from some toys on the floor and ran to an inner room. 'Father's come,' he shouted excitedly to Chieko. The words echoed strangely back to Jun as the boy ran up again to him.

'Why didn't you come sooner?' he demanded in his high voice. 'Come and see my new helicopter.'

He took Jun's hand and pulled him forward. Jun was helpless to resist, the sticky palm was tiny within his own. It took some moments before Chieko came and the child chattered happily. Standing above him, Jun looked down upon his small head and delicate neck. His ears were large, his hands grubby about the helicopter. For the first time then he saw the child was a separate entity in himself, devoid of calculation or the games that adults play; he had not asked to be born. He was no more than a small trusting smile; his son in spite of all. Against his will Jun smiled back, and something broke within him, something tight and painful. The child reached up and pulled him by the hand, he bent on a knee beside it, and began awkwardly to explain the action of propellers as the child listened. He knew then he could never desert the boy, knew then too in one far-sighted, horrible flash to just what extent the woman had trapped him. He looked up and found her watching from a doorway, satisfaction in her eyes.

The next time he came too late, the child was in bed. He stared down at Yukio's sleeping face, innocent of even childish guile. He sighed and turned away. She had gone before him into the living room and had a drink ready. He shook his head and walked to the door, but she pulled him back. He was tired, and sat down without argument and did not refuse the drink. He allowed her to give him another, then leaned back on the sofa, relaxed by the liquor, and the confusion he felt in this apartment. The daylight outside had faded, Chieko did not put on a light, they were silent in the shadows. She leaned forward then across him, her hair touched his cheek. On her breath he smelled the whiskey and knew from before its taste on her tongue. Slowly she placed her lips upon him and her hands upon his body. He meant to resist, he made an attempt, but her will was stronger than his. And every old need and memory of her rose up to conspire against him. He gave up and turned himself roughly upon her. And once the thing was done it seemed to make no difference then if it was occasionally, never or always. He had already broken Kate's every trust. It made no difference now.

In the car now he lifted his head from his hands. Rain speckled the windscreen and blurred the lights of the road before him. There was the smell of damp leaves and the smell of drink upon his breath. His life wound tightly about him, his head ached and his pulse throbbed. There was no escape and no way to live but to collude with his own deceit. It seemed the past had matured and swallowed the present and bit into the future besides. He no longer asked where it might end.

6

Tomorrow she was going home. She tried to accept the death of the child. *Shikata ga nai.* It cannot be helped. It was what they told her, what they all said. She listened to the words that were applied so easily here to every blighted hope, and could not absorb their simple strength. In the day it was easier to carry the emptiness, heavy as a weight. But in the shadows of the darkening room and the fitful dreams of night, the child's small face rose before her again. She could not then in the morning comprehend the meaning of those swollen months behind, or that unbelievable pain that should have been both an end and a beginning. It all lay in her mind like a strange, dark country she had visited and returned from.

At the window now the afternoon was warm and yellow, but she was full of the dread of returning home, to the small, white room with its drawers of little knitted garments and its lamp like a bunch of balloons. She remembered again the tiny appliquéd apron in Fumi's chest, and the thought cut through her painfully. She looked at her watch and then at the silent hospital door, Paula, who had promised to visit, was late. Kate picked up her book and continued to read, of an ancient, illicit world, from that old volume *The Nightless City*.

* *The Nightless City* by J.E. de Becker anonymously published in 1899; edition by Charles E. Tuttle Company Inc. published 1971.

'Chopped burdock root fried in sesame oil. Cuttlefish and lotus root. *Sayori* fish tied in a knot. Salted fern shoots and river mushrooms, etc, all of which foods are suitable for persons who stop in brothels for several consecutive days.

'Organised sex has always been big business in Japan, and nowhere was it more politely offered than in the Yoshiwara Yukwaku, the red light district of Tokyo, a small walled city within the city. The Yoshiwara was established in 1617, and thrived until the disapproval of Western ethical standards after the Second World War, led to its abolition in 1957.

'The family pattern of old Japan was highly polygamous, explicitly allowing a man who could afford it any number of official mistresses. The Japanese attitude to sexual pleasure is traditionally uninhibited. Japanese wives accepted their husband's liaisons with courtesans and prostitutes without complaint.

'Yoshiwara life on the surface was bright, but inmates were virtually slaves. Geisha and courtesans only were allowed beyond the walls on certain days, surveillance was prisonlike and there was corporal punishment for breach of rules.

'Romantic love was greatly disapproved of both at home and in the Yoshiwara as a disruptive influence. Geisha and courtesans who fell in love with clients had to be purchased out of service by their lovers or agree to end the affair or enter into a suicide pact as an honourable end to their shame.

'No samurai was allowed to enter a brothel wearing a sword ... it was well known that some of the women inside would put an end to their lives if they could get hold of a weapon.

Every now and then a woman of gentle birth would be guilty of a lapse of virtue and in order that the stern code of samurai honour might be vindicated she would be sent to the public stews for a term of three or even five years as exemplary punishment for her immoral behaviour.

'Only the very best houses of the Yoshiwara did not exhibit their women. But before the majority the women sat, displayed in vermilion barred cages, exposed to view as living samples, engaged in nothing so crass as whoring, but rather in 'selling Spring'.

'On a calm Spring evening, when the women of the quarter enter their cages it seems as if flowers were being scattered in the Yoshiwara by the bell announcing nightfall. The main avenue at night is lighted by thousands of lanterns, the cherries are in bloom, a great row of them planted down the centre of the Yoshiwara from the main gateway.

'The naming of courtesans: Faint Clouds. Little Purple. Fragrance. Nine Folded. Floral Fan. Pine Mountain. Flower Willow. Little Sleeve.

'A woman wishing to become a courtesan or a prostitute must send a written petition to the police station of jurisdiction. Included must be a document of consent signed and sealed by applicant's father and mother.

'When a first class prostitute was sick a brothel master might go to much expense to cure her and even pray at the temple for her recovery. A lower class girl was merely entrusted to a quack and thrust into some gloomy room.

'A letter to *The Japan Times* 1899. Sir ... if misery, starvation and vicious habits drive women in other countries to immoral calling, here we must add the mistaken motive of filial piety ... because some women will sell their bodies and inhuman parents sell their daughters, does not justify the state making a percentage per year per girl as at present.

'The only affection a respectable man might show his wife was the affection of a master for a domestic pet. Romantic love was considered an effeminate emotion and offended the canons of masculine superiority. The function of women was differentiated into woman as domestic manager and breeder and woman as charming plaything, in the separate personalities of wife and concubine. Thus was a woman divided upon her separate selves and a man master of her divided parts.'

The door opened and Paula appeared.

'I thought you'd never come,' said Kate, and put the book down.

'This wretch was told to wait on the swings for me after school, but naturally was nowhere to be seen.' Paula shook the firmly clasped hand of her small son James. 'You look better, even a smile. That's good.'

The room was all movement now, all Paula. Firm, strong voice, well-fleshed bones, sandy, freckled solidity. Immediately it was a different world that Kate entered with relief. Paula sat down and began a recounting of her universe.

'Oh,' Paula said, 'many things have changed in just the few years we've been away. As you know we're back in the same company house. It's a historic old house and we find we're now one of the sights on the tourist route around Kitano-cho, and the *Ijinkan* houses, those quaint houses built by the early foreigners here in Kobe. We have to lock our doors you know. I feel like something in a zoo. We add exotic colour to the area, I suppose. Real life foreigners in real old foreign houses.'

The world seemed comfortable now to Kate, a place in which she fitted and where even the unpredictable was not entirely unknown. She leaned back upon the pillows and let Paula's gossip fall about her like warm sun. She called James to her and gave him one of Itsuko's oranges.

'Wow. So big. Where d'you get 'em?' His eyes grew round.

'My mother-in-law.'

'The old witch?'

'James!' Paula exclaimed in horror.

'Well, you call her that, Mom. I've heard you.'

'James ... look, why don't you go down to those machines in the entrance and get yourself a drink.'

'O.K. Money.' The door shut behind him.

'*The old witch!* I must learn to keep my mouth shut. Did she come?' Paula asked.

'Yes. Never been more attentive,' Kate reported as brightly as she could. 'Even peeled me an apple.'

'Well. That's a change.'

'Not really. She's just glad the baby died.' Kate spoke bitterly. 'Jun can't seem to stand up to her at all.'

'I should think she's enough to silence anyone,' Paula exclaimed.

'If he would only be firm, and have it out once and for all. But he won't.' Kate admitted.

'I'm sure he would like to. He can't enjoy seeing you suffer. But he's in a difficult position. No wife traditionally expected affection from her husband, she demanded it from her son as a substitute for everything she never had from her marriage. Here a man can ignore his wife, but no man can ignore his mother.'

'But I can't live like she wants me to. Jun *must* make her see.'

'Kate, listen. By refusing to stand up to her, he's not showing weakness, as you think. He's showing strength and virtue. That's how it's seen here. He has a special obligation to his mother, a kind of limitless debt of love which is different from our idea of love as something given freely and unfettered. That's the meaning of filial piety, that places parents in such authority over children. A child must always strive to repay that debt. Jun can't speak up as you want against Itsuko, it's unthinkable.'

'I don't understand it, any of it. I don't understand why they don't break out of their places,' Kate said sullenly.

'Well, it's not that everyone accepts things contentedly, terrible resentments steam below the surface, sometimes with terrible results. Nothing is done directly. There is always a go-between, a third party to negotiate, so that nobody need openly lose face. *Face* and *place*. There, I've summed it all up for you.' Paula laughed.

There was a sudden noise outside the room.

'I didn't do it Mom. I swear I didn't do it.' James appeared in the doorway held firmly by a nurse.

'James, what have you done now?' Paula started up.

'He's tried to break the soft drinks machine. He was hitting the glass window in it with a metal object. I saw him.' The nurse said tartly.

James, did you do that?'

'No, Mom ... I swear I ...'

'But she saw you, she says.'

'Well, I hate the horrid machine. Everything is written in Japanese and I cant understand it and I lost my money.' James yelled, red in the cheeks.

'James! Wait with Kate, I'm going with the nurse to see.' Paula's face was flushed and angry. James sobbed loudly, his eyes defiant.

'James,' said Kate when Paula was gone. 'Come here and let me wipe your nose. Why did you do a thing like that?'

'Told you. Cause I hate the machine. Cause I hate everything here.' James sniffed morosely.

'But why? It's a beautiful country and your school is so nice.' Unused to small children, Kate sounded condescending.

'Well, I hate it. Everyone stares at me all the while, real rude.'

'But when they stare James, they're just curious, you look different from them. They only look in a friendly way.'

'They don't, they laugh and say rude things about me.'

'I'm sure they don't mean anything rude James.'

'Well, I hate it. And I hate school. And I hate being a third culture kid. I haven't any friends. Why can't Mom and Pop go home. Why do we have to live in all these different countries?'

'A third culture kid? What's that James?' Kate asked in puzzlement.

'Aw, what would you know? What would you understand?' James said scathingly, and turned to the wash basin in the room, turning the taps on and off.

'James ... James,' Paula rushed in and yanked James from the basin, 'I am fed up with you, James Bailey. Just wait until your father hears about this. Now they've been real nice about that machine downstairs. In any other country you would be in serious trouble. Now, you come downstairs with me and apologise.' James stuck out his lower lip and looked down at his shoes. Paula turned to Kate and raised her eyes despairingly.

'You'll be leaving the hospital tomorrow, I'll phone you at home in the evening.' She turned out of the door dragging James behind her. The room fell suddenly silent.

Kate took up the book again and read. 'In the winter of 1872, all prostitutes and geisha engaged in brothels throughout the country were unconditionally set free. The losses sustained by the nation's brothel keepers at this time were enormous. However, through debts and circumstances, the unfortunate women were compelled to apply for new licenses to continue their calling in the brothels, now renamed *kashi zashiki*, a house with rooms to let.

'Letter to *The Japan Times* 1899.

'Sir ... if the authorities decide to prohibit the present system of exhibiting women in cages, it will mean men will be obliged to enter the houses in cold blood for a definite purpose, and not be exposed to the temptation of being drawn in by a pretty face on sale ...'

Kate put down the book. That illicit world of the past somehow plunged her back into the present, into all the strangeness of the world that had enclosed her. There was nothing of Paula now left in the room. The last, thin sun of the afternoon settled into greyness. On the wall a glossy calendar showed a Zen temple drawn into mountain pines and mist. Itsuko's oranges stood in a bowl beside the bed. Out in the bay a ship honked mournfully, a dog howled in reply. Paula would sooner or later return to the security of known things.

But she, Kate saw now, was adrift. She had lost the past and could not see a future. She could never again wholly belong to that world Paula carried with her. She had closed the door upon herself that autumn day in Paula's flat, when they had tried their best to warn her. It was clear to her now she was alone, and Jun unable to help her. She drew back then in the bed in fear and listened to the dog reply once more to the mournful ship.

7

Itsuko sat like a small, nesting bird on the floor of a bare, matted room. Shadow dissolved the beams of the ceiling, before her the garden dwindled to evening landscape. At this time the smell of moss and wood reflected the past warm day. It was unseasonably mild. There was the sweetness of damp undergrowth, somewhere in the dusk Fumi watered the garden; a wet pattering upon dry leaves in the fading day, the paleness of her apron moved beyond the trees, from the pool came the rhythmic clack of the mortar. Itsuko stirred and touched her hair, she felt a restful strength in the absence of the bitterness that had consumed her these past months.

The glass doors of the veranda were drawn back, the garden seemed to fill the room. Beyond bamboo thickets the moon hung huge, red as blood, close enough to touch. Itsuko stared at it unswervingly and knew it was an omen. She had no doubt the present events were arrangements of the Gods. Why else was the child dead? She was certain now what she must do; at last she saw the way.

From the porch came the sound of Jun's arrival, and Fumi's greeting as she followed behind him into the house. She had returned that morning from her hospital duty, there was no longer a need for her there. She bent as Jun removed his shoes and turned them neatly, ready for departure, her voice as she spoke to him of Kate was full of concern. Listening, Itsuko felt her exclusion. In the darkness she drew down the corners of her mouth at her sister's sudden loquacity. Fumi's face seemed always waiting to offer a part of itself and filled Itsuko with repugnance. She could see her now through the open door. Crumbs of dry leaf stuck to Fumi's hair, a wet patch where the hose had burst its joint flooded the front of her apron. Her clothes were loose and undistinguished, there was a wrinkle in her stocking. Watering the garden should be left to a servant, but no amount of prompting ever changed her. It was a mystery to Itsuko how this sister could differ so, from either herself or Yoko.

'You're late. It's nearly time,' Itsuko told Jun as he bowed before her. 'What took you so long?'

'I had to go home to feed the cat.'

'A man in your position having to feed a cat.' Itsuko gave a snort followed by a fastidious shudder, her voice opaque with disgust. The animal too was hardly worthy of the name of cat, a wretched creature Kate had snatched from death under the wheels of a car. Bony, diseased and riddled with worms, she still settled it in her home.

'If she would employ a live-in maid there would be no need for you to feed a cat. A part-time maid is gone when she's needed most,' Itsuko pointed out.

'She's not used to maids. She feels her privacy lost with someone always in the house.' He did not add that the maid sent to them by Itsuko, carried with her all the curiosity of the main house.

'We are spied upon,' Kate insisted, 'it is your mother's way of keeping track,' and would have no more to do with the woman. She turned instead to an agency of part-timers Paula recommended.

'Privacy?' Itsuko was amazed. It was not a concept she was familiar with, its provision was not included in her way of life. 'Another strange, imported idea. If she wants to suffer, then it's her affair. But why should you be made to turn a hand to such domestic things? It's neither right nor manly.'

'I don't wash dishes, Mother,' Jun wearily explained. 'We had better switch on the television, or we'll miss the interview.'

Fumi hurried to turn on the set and they all settled before it. They waited and soon in the brilliant square Jun saw his own face stare at him, the face of a stranger, the voice unrecognisable. On the screen beside him was his mother, her expression admitting nothing, exuding social etiquette with small inclinations of the head and the delicacy of her words.

The interview had taken place some days before for a women's hour programme on the local network. Jun's business opinions were sometimes sought by journalists, but it was his mother who attracted attention. She was a Nagai, and that stood for much even in her husband's day within inner business circles. Her name was known beyond spheres of work for she was all but alone in her position in Japan, as an active, powerful woman in industry. As such she was championed by fledgling women's groups and interviewing journalists. Through domestic days in countless little houses women stopped the stirring of a pan and heard or read her name. Itsuko Nagai.

'Do you think of the achievements of your life as being the kind of ideal for modern Japanese women?' a young woman asked.

'In my own lifetime the position of women in Japan has changed in an undreamed of way. But there are women now, who would have us ape some kind of Westernised freedom, although this, thank goodness, is not yet widespread. The average Japanese woman still feels her place firmly in the home. This is as it should be. I believe most women see their strength and power more truly there than in other roles, with their imported ideas of emancipation. I myself believe in the strength of all our traditional virtues. I do not like the erosions I see. I believe they have weakened our identity. I have said many times and I shall say it again, I have not chosen my present role in life from any elevated notion, from any wish to expand my place as a woman. Rather the opposite, it was from that strict observance of my traditional place, in obedience to my husband, that made me determined to devote myself to his memory with the same single-mindedness as when he lived. Until his death, I had taken no active part in the business. I see only total disaster, total social confusion ahead if we abandon our traditional roles.' On the screen Itsuko's eyes were firm beneath soft words.

'But you have now a foreign daughter-in-law. Will this not bring about some change within the family? Did you oppose your son's marriage?' The interviewer addressed herself to Itsuko, but the camera settled on Jun. Now he watched his own anxiety reflect again in that strange face. Itsuko did not stumble, her smooth voice remained unchanged, she smiled.

'There are some evolutions I cannot oppose, the world is a very small place nowadays, there will be more and more of these marriages. But I have always thought we understand far more about the West than the average Westerner knows about Japan.

As such I look forward to teaching my new daughter-in-law our customs and attitudes. We should not always think we must learn from the West. There is much they can learn from us. This is a unique opportunity within the heart of my family.'

Even now she took his breath away, even now he must admire her. How she turned the rough into the smooth, the wayward to her purpose. On the screen Itsuko's lips moved easily in reply to other questions. Jun listened to her elegant replies, and it struck him now for the first time, how avidly she guarded her own domain. How, having found her own strengths and freedom, she would deny other women the same. Before the war her position would have been unthinkable, whatever her abilities. It was precisely the Westernised trends she proposed to condemn that allowed her to be what she was. He felt the heat of annoyance at such hypocrisy. Beside her he appeared on the screen ineffectual and received little attention. But soon brash advertisements ended the interview and when the programme continued, a cookery demonstration replaced them. Jun switched off the television and the room retreated behind the glow of a table lamp.

Itsuko patted her hair and adjusted her neck within the collar of her kimono, her mind still full of the image of her own face. Amidst dewy colour and commercialism it had remained something separate and contained. Unlike that pert little interviewer with her endless, calcified smile. Satisfaction animated Itsuko's small frame, she thought she came out of it all very well.

Immediately Fumi began to bustle, hurrying up old Hirata-*san* in the serving of their dinner. She began to fuss about Jun, like an anxious hen.

'See,' she said, 'I have made sea bream today in your favourite way. Especially for you. I knew you'd like it.' She giggled at Jun's pleasure, eyes bright and tender. Her hands, settling the many small dishes before him, changing slightly their positions, pulling the pickles nearer for convenience, fluttered unashamedly affectionate.

Itsuko stared coldly, but Fumi seemed not to see. Chose not to see, thought Itsuko. It was always like this, everyday, every meal. It had begun when Fumi came back to live in the old house after Itsuko's husband died. Almost at once she established a bond with the young Jun. They spoke in corners, warm laughing glances were exchanged and the perplexities of adolescence Jun carried to his aunt. In the beginning Itsuko tried not to notice, but bad dreams shredded nights and drove into her day. She could not look at her sister's plain and kindly face. For a good part of that first year together she refused to speak to Fumi, who for months entreated to know the reason. Itsuko kept her silence deliberately, but she told her at last in the autumn, while viewing the maples in Kyoto.

In the Kiyomizu Temple they had stood together at the edge of the huge stage of the *hondo* that hung out in the air upon massive supports. The great shingled roof towered above and the famous vista, crimson with maples, was clear before them as if they stood upon a mountain top. It came out of her mouth at last then, like a round, hard, bitter stone.

'You've stolen my son.'

She heard Fumi's shocked silence, clear as the call of a bird above them. 'You have lost your own and would now steal mine.'

Fumi went rigid and had not said a word.

As she spoke then, memories flowed back into Itsuko, so that she reached out and gripped the rail before her. For she remembered that other time many years before, when she had come to the temple to pray to the Kiyomizu's eleven-faced, thousand-armed *kannon*, for the easy birth of a son. Her husband had been with her then, and they had stood exactly there, looking out across Kyoto. Few words, she remembered, passed between them. It was winter then and before them all Kyoto seemed as frugal and bare and brown as the temple's weathered, wooden structure, a strong wind whistled in their ears. A son, she had prayed, a son and heir. Beside her she knew her husband willed the same hard wish. She had heard in the past peasant women in birth closed their thighs upon girl children, or drowned them within minutes. And she had understood, for she knew already the shame the birth of a girl would bring her; both her husband and father waited for a son.

Even the husband who had stood beside her, adopted as her father's heir was not free of that affliction. The obligatory bonds placed upon him as an adoptive husband, behooved him for life to a special burden. In private he spoke bitterly to Itsuko of the resentments he felt, but could never indulge. He became a morose and silent man, and once she had safely borne a son and had the status of a mother, she allowed herself to despise him. He turned for comfort to debauchery, taking as mistress a famous geisha, whom he set up in an establishment of her own. Itsuko's heart had filled with violence, but there was nothing she could do, it was her duty to accept. He did no more than live the established pattern for a man of substance, a traditional townsman in every way. He did no more than her own father, and his father too before him. Itsuko was merely a wife; her small sphere was ringed and fenced, what happened beyond her little plot could be no concern of hers. Itsuko put her memories behind her, and turned away from the television towards the table. When she remembered the interview some balance seemed righted. She lifted the lid of a lacquer container and began to serve the rice.

'The fish is so good,' Jun praised Fumi. 'I've not had sea bream like this for years.'

'I went to the market on the way home from the hospital, I wanted to surprise you. Hirata-*san* had already begun something different, she's upset with me for changing her menu. But I made it for you myself in just the way you like,' Fumi laughed.

'Delicious,' Jun shook his head and took another bite.

Itsuko averted her eyes from the gentle game they played together. She tried to control the feelings that began to stir in her. It was not fair, it was not right. Jun was *her* son, it was she who had nursed him until he was four, and could no longer sit comfortably upon her lap. But even after that he had slept until quite big beside her in her bed; his father had slept in a separate room. His hand had often stolen to fondle in sleep her bare breast beneath her kimono. Yet even that intimacy between them had not brought the easy affection Fumi seemed immediately to procure. A cold, tight jealousy filled her.

Often in their childhood she had felt this way about Fumi. They had been brought up in this old house. For as long as Itsuko could remember she had eaten at this table, sat each evening in this room. Its wooden beams in the ceiling above had looked down on each hour of her life, each pain and dream. It was an introverted house full of dark corners. Trees fenced in three sides, shutting out the sun that filtered through in a dark, green light. At night the trees stirred and murmured against the shuttered windows. Often, as a child, Itsuko woke and felt the restless melancholy of the place. In the dark it seemed to fill and claim her. She listened to the rustling trees and the waterfall that fell forever behind the house and strange thoughts and violent feelings filled her. Once, she remembered still, turning to look at little Fumi asleep on a futon beside her. The darkness obscured Fumi's face but the moon cut in a blade across her throat. Itsuko rose on an elbow and stared, and a terrible feeling had filled her. The same passion for hate as when secretly, she pulled the wings of insects from their helpless bodies. She lay back, and the feeling had throbbed in her, louder than the stirring leaves.

The sense of direction in her now was sharp as that blade of light so long ago upon Fumi's throat. Already the solid mass of confusion confronting her these past months was gone. The future lay in her to mould, she was impatient to begin. Itsuko could not remember a single incident in her life that was not eventually arranged as she wished. She simply closed herself upon ambition until within her body there was no break, not the breadth of a hair, between what she willed and what would happen. For the first time now since Jun's marriage, she was sure it was not too late.

Jun accepted a bowl of rice from his mother, but did not meet her gaze. A strange, distracted energy seemed to come from her this evening. Her glance was preoccupied, a cold vivacity brimmed in her eyes. He had seen that look on her face before and knew some dubious mechanism had begun to work within her. And as soon as the meal was finished, he noticed she found a reason to be rid of Fumi, so that they sat alone.

The room still held the warm spring evening and the earthy smell of the garden. The moon hung red in the branches of the loquat tree, a moth fluttered against the window. The light of a low standing lamp filled the room, Itsuko faced Jun across the table, her hands cupped about a bowl of tea.

'So, *she* comes home tomorrow.' Never once had she used Kate's name. Jun nodded. 'Some women have not the talent for children,' Itsuko noted meditatively.

'She just did too much after we moved and emotionally, settling is difficult for her. Everything is strange, all these things have played a part. There will be other times, other children,' Jun repeated Fumi's words.

'Perhaps we will always seem strange to her. Perhaps she will never settle,' Itsuko softly observed. In the low light of the room an emerald flashed upon her hand.

'You must give her time. It was the same for me when I went to London. It was not just another country; it was another world. It was not until I met Kate that I learned a truer understanding.'

Itsuko raised an eyebrow. 'It seems you have understood so well you have forgotten your own heritage,' she replied.

Itsuko held up a hand as Jun protested. 'No, tonight you must listen to me. I speak only for your good. All these strange ideas you have learned from your wife. I am not saying for her they are wrong. She belongs to a different culture. Do you not understand your position? Some day you will sit where I am. She is not the right wife. Not the right wife for a man in your position. She has divided and confused you.' Itsuko was adamant.

'Your views, Mother, are not part of today's world. The Japan we live in is very different from the Japan you were brought up in.' He dared to tell her, the words fighting angrily in him.

'As far as I am concerned very little has changed for the better. We had strong guidelines then that are sadly lacking today. But we are the same nation, the same people with the same belief in ourselves. Our strength and direction has not altered, only our vocabulary.'

'But I have *married* her,' Jun stated, angrily.

'Well,' said Itsuko, suddenly and softly, her voice dropping as she leaned across the table. 'You can unmarry her. You can divorce her. You can marry again, a more suitable match. It's not too late, not with our position and wealth.'

'Mother!' He started back on his cushion, shocked.

'Yes,' she said, not seeming to notice his horror. 'I have thought and thought and this is the way. You made a mistake. You were confused and maybe lonely in London. I am also to blame, I should have insisted you marry, long before. I should not have listened to you. In the old days as you well know, I would have had the authority to dissolve your marriage, even expel you from the family for marrying without my permission. Yes, when I think of it now, times have indeed changed.' She laughed, not unkindly, animated by all she was saying, and the power it seemed to give her.

'But we live in modern times, as you say. And I am not one to push my authority. I just ask you to seriously consider my proposal. There is no need for shame, there are several valid reasons to put forward to the world. She is a foreigner, everyone will understand. Her unsuitability, and inability to adjust can be stressed. It is not your fault, you will not be blamed. It is for your good, and hers. I do not think she will ever settle.' Itsuko pulled back across the table and regarded her son gravely, watching the weight of her words upon him.

'Mother,' he leaned forward determinedly. 'I love her, I want no other wife.' Even to say it to her, so nakedly, made him curl inside. How could she ever understand how he had met and married Kate?

'Love?' She laughed incredulously behind her hand. 'You are not a woman. What is love compared to duty? Have you forgotten everything to which you were born? What has this woman done to you? Love? Where is your strength of will?'

He wondered, beneath his throbbing pulse, what Kate would make of this conversation if she could overhear. How could she ever understand that to his mother's way of thinking the pursuit of personal happiness as a goal in life was both amazing and immoral. The strength of will that duty required was all that mattered to her. They were not a nation of "happily-ever-afters". Heroes here were not rewarded by earthly happiness for virtue. Lovers gave up love for duty and came to tragic but virtuous ends. Happy couples committed suicide in the proper performance of duty. Weak feelings must never come between a man and his obligations.

'Love,' his mother considered the word and then continued. 'Tell me, what will this mean to your wife when she knows of your *other* love?' Her eyes were dark now and wily as she laid her trump card in the space between them. It was as if she hit him, she saw his whole body contract. 'What will all this love you talk of mean to her then?'

'That was something of the past, as you well know. And something quite different to what there is between Kate and I. It was before I met her. I was a different person then.' He spoke stiffly, in a low voice. 'She must never know.'

'It is very difficult to keep a secret like that. How long can it be before she hears in one way or another?'

'Who will tell her?' He had never thought she would bring this up, stoop to this kind of blackmail.

'Certainly not I, rest assured. But it is something beyond yourself. It is a risk you will always live with. And Chieko is the jealous type, clever too. And what then? Your wife will not understand in the way a Japanese woman would. What then of this great love of yours?' He did not reply.

It was enough. She sat back, and drew new breath, and poured herself more tea. She had planted her seeds, but looking at Jun she felt a sudden rush of warmth at the despondence in his face. She did not wish always to appear a jailer, but life had cast her as custodian of the lives about her. It was her duty to inflict these disciplines that later he would be grateful for. She gave him a bowl of tea and sighed before their combined and uncertain fate.

'Come. It is for your good that I say these things. I would not be your mother if I did not worry for your welfare. Think about what I have said, there is no hurry. I feel you have made a grave mistake, but there is this way out. It is not too late. And I suspect even now, she might gladly go home if you gave her the opportunity. She is not happy here, she will never adjust.'

Jun stood up, the bowl of tea untouched and left the room without a goodbye. Itsuko followed and stood staring after him as he closed the door.

When he had gone she did not go back to the *tatami* room but turned instead into her Western-style lounge. The room was for visitors, not for everyday use. It lay out of bounds in a solitary, shuttered confinement only Itsuko was allowed to break. Here the upright world of furniture was like an island in the low eye levels of the house. Here a raised-work velvet couch and chairs were part of a prim, stiff land of polish and glass and antimacassars and a candle chandelier. An arrangement of spring flowers stood between a large portrait of Itsuko and a copy of Utrillo's *Église de Saint-Mamert.* Itsuko sat down in a chair and sadly smoothed an antimacassar over a velvet arm. Her portrait always brought her here at times of trouble or confusion, and she turned in the chair to gaze up at it. Within its painted likeness she found a comfort the mirror now refused to give. The picture had been painted by a well-known artist soon after she was married. The strange flat style blended the patterns of Itsuko's kimono into the thick, dark foliage of the background. From these soft shapes and colours her face stared out like a pale bloom, exotic and untouchable; her own mystery seemed to possess her. The portrait appeared with magnificent assurance to fix her, ageless, upon the plane of time. She never tired of its reflection, and looked at it again now, seeking reassurance. She found it always in the painted image of her own eyes, and knew again her way was right.

Jun drove aimlessly for a while when he left his mother, restless and disturbed. He could not face the thought of home. He had no intention of going to the place until he found himself before the door. The bar was one in Kobe he often patronised, a high-class establishment where they knew him well. It was here, long before, that he had met Chieko. The madame herself came forward as he entered, a woman in her fifties, well past the demands of easy virtue, now established respectfully in her trade.

'Well, well. I thought you had forgotten us. How many weeks has it been?' She smacked him playfully on the arm once the formal bows were finished. 'Only last night the girls were wondering what could have become of Nagai-*san*. It's that foreign wife of yours. She holds a short rein and your pleasures are ended.' She laughed up at him, her face a round, smooth bubble of paint and affectation.

Sachiko and Yumi freed themselves from noisy groups of men and came across the room to fuss playfully about him. He allowed them to lead him to a table. The madame too sat down with them, a drink and snacks were placed before him. Sachiko offered him a cigarette and lit it for him. Yumi stroked his sleeve.

'Such a long time. We were lonely.'

The low lights in the room reflected the pink decor, there was the glint of glass and the girls' moist eyes and their flesh, exposed and white. The hard shapes of things dissolved within the soft décor with its insinuations of sensuality. A rainbow light revolved above the bar, changing the women's bare skin to strange unearthly hues. Jun took a long drink of the whiskey before him and felt his mother's face recede.

A group of business executives in the middle of the room argued boisterously and the women sitting with them, expert in the thrust and parry of words, changed potential arguments into jokes or ribald exchanges, until the men were relaxed and the tensions of the day eased. It was unlike the lonely, impersonal drinking Jun had found abroad. He smiled at the women.

'Only yesterday Chieko came to visit us. She always comes back to me for advice, tells me I'm like her mother. Of course I have an interest in my girls, even after they leave me. I care what happens to them. We talked about you, about old times,' the madame told him, sipping a drink. Although he had met Chieko here, nobody knew of his relationship with her, he had sworn her to silence. But it was through the bar she had heard of his marriage. He assumed innocence and nodded, asking how Chieko was.

'All right, but not too happy. It seems her patron is difficult. And you know she has a child now.'

The drink worked through him, he had not to think of Kate tonight, waiting accusingly at home. She could never understand this side of life here, or the part it played in society. The evening was before him, and he accepted another drink. His mother's face was far away and Kate's soon also faded. He put an arm along the back of Yumi's chair. Sachiko's cool fingers withdrew from his lips a stub of cigarette and prepared to light him another. Soon he would tell them of his sadness about the baby, and listen to their sympathy. The groups of men began to blur before him. Something unwound within him that had been tight for days.

It was late when he got home. The cat waited, bony and resentful before the closed front door. He greeted it with distaste and watched it bound ahead of him into the empty house. It seemed to make Kate happy and for that reason he tolerated it. Upstairs he lay down fully dressed upon the bed, his mind woollen with drink. Now he was home Kate filled his mind again. He thought of her in the nursing home, and remembered his mother's wily words. Just the thought of Kate now fragmented him, made him live upon two planes. He must fit again the requirements of his past, and yet marriage to Kate and his life abroad had changed him. He had never forgotten, as his mother supposed, that he was a Nagai, nor the virtue of his

Japanese ways, but he had lived a strange duality. The confusion exhausted him. Behind his closed eyes the world revolved nauseatingly. He pulled himself up and switched on the bedside light. Beyond the open door of the room Kate had prepared for the child. There was the basket cradle she had lined with lace, the chest of tiny knitted feet, bloomers, hats and diapers, all the peripheral features of a child that had not come to them. How could he ever tell her that destiny had already made him a father? He thought then of that other child he would never call his own. His mother's words came back to him and filled his mind with fear. There was no knowing what she schemed. That secret part of his life was shut off somewhere deep within him, separate from the flow of things, and silence lay upon it. He prayed Kate would never know.

8

The room combined the pomp of cathedrals and circuses. Encrustments of mirrors and chandeliers reflected light. A garish modern tapestry hung above a forest of men in dark suits. There were three hundred guests, all of them men. Apart from three geisha and the waitresses, the only woman was his mother. Jun watched her across the banqueting hall of the hotel. About him the room was brilliant, as Itsuko had planned. A large placard outside the room announced "Centenary Celebration of Nagai Spinning Mill". There were pictures below of the mill at the turn of the century, great drab sheds, surrounded by a squalid huddle of wooden huts and roofs that were the suburbs of Osaka.

Beside this was a photo of the present modern mill, bordered by the paranoia of industrial activity that now made up Osaka. Jun greeted the president of an electronics company and over his shoulder caught sight once more of Nubuo Tamura standing with a plate of food beside a knot of men, and embarrassment filled him again. He could not understand what made his mother invite Tamura, it was hardly politic. Itsuko only wished to flaunt herself before him. He was surprised Tamura had even come. Recently they had been awarded by the government, in preference to Tamura, the whole export quota of yarn to Senegal. They heard many rumours afterwards of how Tamura smarted, and they knew his dubious ways from long ago. What good would it do to antagonise him with their superior success? He saw his mother had seen Tamura and made her way towards him.

Tamura stood across the room, his face already flushed by drink. Itsuko Nagai approached him, like a small, bright bird of prey. Her eyes if they could would have petrified the corpulent form before her. They bowed and Itsuko, observing the proper etiquette in the depth and length of bow, was careful to lower herself less than the man before her. In this manner they straightened with identical timing, saving a further performance.

'How good of you to come.' Her words were whetted as a pebble. The plate he had collected from the buffet tipped in Tamura's embarrassed hand, some salmon fell to the floor.

'Careful.' Itsuko put out a hand and straightened the plate with a little laugh, and the sound whipped the blood to Tamura's face. She was without charity. Tamura coughed a cough that did not deceive. He flushed deeper in annoyance above the congratulations he was obliged to offer again.

Long before he had worked for Itsuko's husband, but leaked important information to a rival enterprise. He left in disgrace but never forgot the slur this cast upon him. By accepting a leftover spinster as wife, he married into money. His contacts were many and dubious. He made his first wealth through the occupation and then by supplying dried blood plasma to American forces in Korea. A few *yen*, and a meal to any vagrant who would donate blood, had been the basis of his wealth. Then came black market tie-ups with the Japanese underworld.

One way or another he rose, outside the aristocracy of money. He dared compete with the haughty Nagais and threaten their monopolies. He was not a man Itsuko cared to be seen with, she was anxious to move on. But not for a moment would she have omitted to ask him to the celebration, not have seen the salmon slip from his plate. Satisfied, she left him for the manager of a bank, and she continued her progress across the room. Her formal, black kimono embroidered with the family crest, had a lavish hem with designs of peonies and birds. The bronze brocade of her *obi* warmed about her like dull metal under the chandeliers. Among the dreary horde of men she was not without splendour. On the back and sleeves of the kimono was the small veined leaf of a paulownia that was the family crest, and she carried it proudly through the room. She had risen to where she was through the fortune of circumstance, but also upon her own merits. She was the only woman in the room, and as she observed the men about her she thought of that great collective army, their married halves. It would be unusual to invite them, and few would anyway choose to come. They led separate social lives from their husbands, bright and active, but safely contained in exclusively feminine meetings. Wherever Itsuko moved men parted and regrouped about her, always respectful of her presence, unsure of how to handle her. She looked about with satisfaction; everyone who should be there had come. The room rippled like a mirror with the reflection of her life.

On the long tables of the buffet light trembled in aspic, silver and glass and the thin glaze upon a pâté. On great platters goggle-eyed, open-mouthed fish, were devoured to their spines.

Roasts of beef and wild boar, and the strange, black eggs of China, preserved it was said for fifty years. Plates of abalone, quail eggs, oysters, and rare mushrooms, no expense had been spared. Itsuko shook her head to a canapé offered by a waiter, this was not the time to eat. She began to make her way to an official from the ministry who had been instrumental in their acquiring that recent quota to Senegal.

The room closed about Jun, palpable and warm. Through windows the sun set in a smear behind the density of the town. Along raised highways the lights of cars melted to a molten stream, red and white, driving West from Osaka along the bay to Kobe, where Kate waited for him.

A group of men pressed about him. The few unfamiliar guests produced at once their visiting cards. Through gaps in the hedge of dark suits he glimpsed at times the three geisha, hired to play and sing, arranged on a dais before their instruments. The angular notes of a *samisen* struck small rents in the hum of conversation. One woman danced, a slow poised turning of head and hands, another sang, moving slightly with emotion beneath a voluminous wig, her throat releasing the words of song in high, contorted notes. And watching them, Jun remembered again the geisha Umeka, who had been his father's last mistress. He heard that when they met she had been sixteen and his father forty-nine. Both his father and his grandfather had been great frequenters of the tea houses.

Tamura was making his way across the room. He stopped first at the buffet to replenish his salmon, and then joined the knot about Jun. Soon the group dispersed and they were alone.

'A splendid event.' Tamura's breath gushed fish. 'My congratulations also on your new invention. I heard it will cut spinning time and cost. How shall we compete with you? But I warn you to be careful. Many competitors will be jealous. You must be careful.' He laughed to himself, a greasy laugh. Jun tried to back away.

'And your mother. Really, she is wonderful, not another woman like her. Who can compete with her? It must be hard for you who have inherited all this. I cannot see her ever retiring.' Tamura warmed. Jun caught the eye of a politician, bowed to Tamura and turned away.

Tamura deposited his plate upon a passing tray, and lit a cigarette. In his hand the sudden spurt of flame was reflected in his spectacles. He sucked from his teeth a fragment of food, then turned unhurriedly to the door. Jun watched him leave in relief.

Soon the room began to clear. The remnants of the evening lay littered in giant ashtrays and dirty plates of half-chewed food. Screwed-up balls of paper napkin and the ash of cigarettes were trampled on the floor. Red-coated waiters hurried about, the geisha packed away their instruments, the last guests bowed and left.

'An evening to remember.' Itsuko congratulated herself in the lift, and bowed her thanks to the geisha who came down and followed behind them as they walked through the lobby to the massive glass doors.

'Will you go and pick her up, or shall I send the car?' Itsuko demanded when they arrived in Kobe, for Kate had gone for the evening to the Baileys. 'Why don't you come home for a while first?'

'It's already late,' Jun excused himself, although it was only nine o'clock. Itsuko nodded and instructed the chauffeur to drive first to Jun's home. There, before the open car door, he bowed formally to his mother, and bowed again as the car drove away before turning to his gate.

In the house he went straight to the phone. 'I'm still in Osaka. It will be later than I thought. Can you wait for me there, at Paula's?' he asked when he heard Kate's voice. He looked at his watch and reckoned he had about two hours. 'About eleven.' He replaced the phone and hesitated a moment before walking out of the house again. It was as if a curtain came down one life and another began, and nothing connected the two. He had simply shut one door and opened another, equally part of himself. In the garage he started the car and prepared to drive to Chieko.

'Nine o'clock and we've not even had dinner.' Paula took a long gulp of her wine. 'He's asleep now. What are we to do with him?' She pushed back her fringe distractedly.

James had that afternoon climbed over the neighbour's wall after a football, and trampled over the precious moss and old stones of that garden. He had been caught in the act by the owner himself, a small, grizzled man who the day before had refused to return James' frisbee to him.

'Oh that child,' Paula moaned again, then laughed. 'It's terrible I know, but I've often thought of the revenge I also might inflict if given the chance upon that disagreeable old man.

'But why is he being so naughty all the time? He wasn't like this before in London,' Kate asked.

'He's unhappy. I guess we're up against the overseas syndrome. Poor kid's lived in so many places.' Pete said.

'But you lived here before, he was all right then,' Kate said. 'He had two good friends then, his own little world. But you know the overseas circuit, everyone moves on after a few years to another posting and James's friends have all gone,' Paula told her.

'Surely he can make more?' Kate asked.

'Oh, enough of James for one day. I'm glad Jun will be late, now we'll have some evening together.' They realised then how hungry they were, and came quickly to the table.

'How was Jun, how was the party?' Pete inquired, filling Kate's wine-glass. 'Did he say anything on the phone?'

'Both fine, I think.' Kate paused on a mouthful of dinner, her mind suddenly thick with resentment again. Pete and Paula exchanged a look above her lowered head.

'Come now, don't feel so bad,' Pete comforted. 'Women simply aren't invited to things like this here.'

'Well, I'm really beginning to know how a Japanese wife feels. There seem to be so many evenings alone,' Kate replied.

'Well, it's not unusual here, you know. The women do stay at home, and expect to. Couples don't lead joint social lives.' Pete told her.

'You should find a job. Get busy.' Paula suggested.

'What about my mother-in-law?' Kate asked, ignoring his last comment.

'Oh *her* !' Paula exclaimed. 'She's not a woman, she's a machine, she's not an average woman in the Japanese sense of the word. Do you know what they call a career woman here? A hysterical woman. Yes. There is still great stigma attached to a woman leaving her rightfully considered place in the home. Few are brave enough to face the scorn. Great numbers of women work part-time of course, but a real career woman is a rare species.'

'Jun seems out as many nights as he's in. There are always so many business people to entertain. Why doesn't he bring them home, I don't mind? But no, they must always go to these bars and places.' The words blew away from her now, rinsed out by the wine and before it a gin.

'It's the way things are done here. Nobody entertains at home. And as for the bar culture, it serves a purpose here. It's the other side of the social rigidity, it's the bridge between work and home. Every man has his bar, it's a Japanese institution, like the English pub!' Pete explained.

'The world of the bars is the modern counterpart of the world of the old teahouses. A lot of business is successfully concluded in bars, as it used to be concluded in the tea houses with geisha acting the same role. As the bar hostess. Jun cannot escape this side of Japanese life.' Paula refilled their wine-glasses and Pete continued to elaborate.

'The conducting of personal relations in Japan is a highly sensitive procedure. All kinds of complicated techniques and delicate explorations are required in business negotiations. Rather like an intricate dance. Things are seldom openly stated. When they have to be, a go-between is used. And the women in these places serve that purpose, They are a kind of mixture of temporary romance, maternal concern, and sympathetic drinking companion. For the men the relationship is casual and unhampered by any overworked intimacy. They just enjoy the flattery and sympathy.'

'I don't need a lecture,' Kate responded.

'It's not the drinking, it's the thought of all those women,' she added.

'The rhythm of life and of relationships is different in every society. Emotional bonds between husbands and wives have their own cultural pattern.'

In London, before they married, Kate remembered they had gone to a performance at the National Theatre of *Romeo and Juliet*. She arrived late and they hurried inside the auditorium, where lights already blazed on renaissance Verona. Afterwards they went for a drink in a nearby pub.

'*Romeo and Juliet* is very popular in Japan,' he told her.

'The theme of double suicide is a very Japanese one. It is used often in our literature and films. The concept of the union of lovers in death is well understood by the Japanese because of the Buddhist philosophy of reincarnation. Fated lovers always think they will be reborn into a better life. The playwright, Chikamatsu, sometimes called our Shakespeare, also wrote a famous play about a double suicide.'

She understood much better now the social inflexibilities behind his explanation. She took another sip of wine as Paula spoke again.

'It's considered very modern now for young people to be in love, but people still rarely marry out of class. Everything depends on place.'

Kate nodded dully. All the Baileys said enlightened but did not encourage her. Instead of opening doors, more appeared, until they surrounded her like a maze. She felt suddenly without defence against a whole land and culture. Japanese women had behind them the narrowness of centuries and the wiles of survival. She saw it in Fumi's pathetic, tender fussing about Jun, the pandering to his every whim, untying his shoelaces, massaging his shoulders. She saw it in Itsuko's crafty control of life, nothing overtly stated, yet every aim fulfilled. She had seen it in Yoko's slim eyes, filled with sensuality and calculation, in the strength to survive by every feminine means. In the end this history of cruel dismissal produced a formidable force of women. At this moment it seemed that Japanese men, pampered and spoilt at home, indulged and milked by pleasure outside, were now the victims of a national conspiracy of women, so that she was not so sure this country, termed the most patriarchal, was not more truly matriarchal in many ways. Perhaps this explained why Japan appeared so misogynist. Whatever the positions and the strengths, it was all part of a sexist game she knew she would never fully grasp or understand. Kate decided she would only survive by being true to her own identity. She looked at her watch, it was past eleven, Jun had not come.

9

Tamura hit his wife across the face, blood welled up where his signet ring caught her on the cheekbone. She made no noise, as usual; just shrank back against the wall, neither standing nor squatting. Only her money had persuaded him to marry her. She was too ugly to draw any suitors, a bag of bones and sinew, thick lips always parted over prominent teeth. The marriage had brought him all he desired; and he hit her again for that.

She shielded her face with an arm and over her elbow her eyes stared at him, small and dark as a vindictive bird. Not unlike that damned Nagai woman, he thought, as she had righted his plate of salmon at her party the day before. He recollected his feelings, his shame and confusion and the congratulations that seemed glued to the roof of his mouth. She had no reason but spite to invite him. And what, he wondered, had possessed him to go? He hit his wife even harder, then wiped his palms on the cotton vest stretched across his belly. His fingers were short and thick as cigar stubs.

'Get out of my sight.' He yelled, and she stumbled forward, nursing her cheek.

'Tell them you fell again,' he hissed. Whether the servants believed this or not was immaterial, the excuse was all that mattered. It was understood that the green and yellow blotches covering his wife were the results of a strange disease that caused her to fall about like a ninepin, though at no time had this been witnessed. She took it all silently; she knew her duty, she knew her place. And what wife did not expect a beating? It kept the balance of roles, he thought.

Matsue shut the door behind her and he sat back on the bed to pull on Tamura's socks. It was already eight in the morning. The beating had exhilarated him, like a good game of golf, or a night with a new woman. He flexed his muscles then observed the clothes she had laid out for him. He did not like the match and yelled again for her. The door opened at once, she could only have been outside, still snivelling he saw, by the dampness about her eyes.

'What's this, *eh*? When have I ever worn this tie with this shirt, this shirt with this suit?' he barked, standing in his underclothes and socks, his belly hanging low before him. Still nursing her cheek, she hurried to the cupboard and lifted out a fresh set of clothes. He observed her as she knelt, the kimono tight about her skinny buttocks, and the gap of brown skin between its hem and top of her white *tabi* sock.

Her family had once maintained with considerable status the wealthiest brothel in Osaka. Her father, a graduate of Tokyo University, had inherited the business from his father along with ample, social pretensions. Open house had often been held, when pillars of the local community were entertained to formal tea ceremony by some of the best tea masters. But American influence ended legal prostitution in 1957 and the underworld took over.

Matsue's father had married his youngest daughter to Sakamoto Yujiro, the son of the boss of a powerful gang.

Matsue, the eldest daughter, long ago shelved for spinsterhood, had been married at last through Sakamoto's connections, to Tamura, who had overlooked her age and plainness for the money that came with her. And by marriage he was the brother-in-law of one of Osaka's most powerful men, for Sakamoto soon succeeded his father to headship of the gang. When at last he set up on his own textile mill with the help of Sakamoto, Tamura began to compete with the haughty Nagais. What could not be achieved by legal means was achieved by fear and extortion. The business soon grew to a large concern, satisfying Tamura and Sakamoto.

Tamura strode from the room and through the house. Three servants waited for him at the bottom of the stairs, and bowed as he rounded the curve in the wrought iron bannisters, and kept it up, huddled together, bobbing like roped geese. In the porch he changed from slippers into shoes and stood for Matsue to tie his laces. She followed him out to the waiting chauffeured car and bowed as he drove away. From huge kennels each side of the gate two Akita dogs pulled on their chains and barked, biting savagely at the air.

Tamura left the concrete edifice of his home and drove to the even larger proportions of Sakamoto's mansion. There, after a closed circuit television certified identity, the massive copper doors rolled back upon a spacious garden. Sakamoto's henchmen littered the place like a variety of crew-cut garden gnomes, standing about in twos and threes waiting for the day.

Sakamoto sat on the floor in a silk dressing gown, gnawing a chicken leg. As Tamura bowed, and uttered greetings, and thanks for support and patronage, a door opened at the far end of the room, and two of Sakamoto's henchmen appeared, supporting between them a further man, who appeared the to have taken a beating, his lip was split and bleeding.

Sakamoto continued to pull at the chicken and spoke through its meaty shreds. 'Men used to offer a finger to atone for offense, but I find it an outmoded custom, we must move with the times. Money is a better means of apology.'

'What did he do?' Tamura asked.

'Women,' said Sakamoto mysteriously, his cheeks greasy with chicken fat.

He put down the bone and a subordinate immediately appeared with a steaming towel. As Sakamoto wiped his fingers, cleaning precisely round each nail, his sleeves fell back upon his short tattooed arms. The whole of his back, buttocks and thighs were covered with a female demon, tattooed in inky blues and reds and a dangerous yellow dye. Sakamoto's skin was like a diaphanous cloth that patterned his naked body. Only once, when they had bathed together at a hot spring resort, where they had gone with a party of women, had Tamura seen this great work of art. Sakamoto was said to have sold his skin to a tattoo museum, Tamura remembered now.

'Well,' said Sakamoto, sitting back upon his cushion. 'Did you bring it all?'

'Yes,' replied Tamura opening his briefcase and placing the wads of notes on the table. 'It's all there.'

'Good.' Sakamoto summoned a henchman to take away the money.

Tamura had trouble at his factory with an agitating union. Sakamoto, for a price, had sent a group of men to 'deal' with the main offenders. Tamura had also sought assistance in keeping the mouths of stockholders shut about troubles he had no wish to explain. Sakamoto's men easily intimidated into respectful silence any shareholders with questions. He snapped the briefcase shut in relief at the final payment of these debts, and accepted a cigar from Sakamoto.

'Whiskey?'

Tamura nodded and took a good gulp as soon as the glass was placed before him. Sakamoto turned his attention to a piece of sirloin steak that had been placed before him. Even at eight-thirty in the morning the room was dark with panelling and velvets. A plaster cast of Venus de Milo stood beneath a huge round lamp of faceted glass, reflective and revolving.

The house was full of henchmen with the traditional crew-cuts of gangsterland or the tight curled perms that were popular now as a mark of modern times. It was all changing, Tamura noted to himself. He wouldn't trust one of these sadistic louts out of sight of Sakamoto.

With an effort Tamura kept his attention on Sakamoto who still concentrated on his steak.

'I've had to close down our project.' Tamura cleared his throat nervously.

'What project?' Sakamoto asked absently, chewing with an open mouth, his lips wet with meaty juice. There were always so many projects.

'The air spinning project.'

'You can't let those Nagais get away with it?' Sakamoto reached for a toothpick and poked about inside his mouth.

'We don't have the right work team, we don't have the right brains,' Tamura admitted despondently.

'What progress are the others making?' Sakamoto asked.

'Almost finished, just upping speeds,' Tamura replied.

'Have they applied yet for a patent?'

'Don't think so,' Tamura shook his head.

'I told you to take some short cuts. You could have stolen the blueprints, you could have been first, but now well ... it's very late.' He withdrew the toothpick from his mouth.

'But there must be something, there must be some way ... I can't think of that woman getting away with it. There'll be no way to contain her arrogance. I can see her face, I can hear her voice.' Tamura broke off, with an effort he lowered his voice.

'I thought maybe you might ...'

Sakamoto's bodyguard entered the room, a huge man with a glass eye and a broken nose. He handed a note to Sakamoto who at once stood up in agitation and began to undo his dressing gown, as if he would finish dressing in the middle of the lounge.

'I must go, some urgent business has come up, said Sakamoto as Tamura looked at him from his cushion on the floor.

'I thought maybe it was not too late, that there might yet be some way, some means ...'

'There are always ways, there are always means. Tell me the way and I'll apply the means.' Sakamoto nodded and left the room.

Tamura cursed softly, drank down the remains of the whiskey and soon went out to his waiting car, his expression dark with thought.

10

Already it was August. It had been more than eight months since she arrived in Japan. Behind her the days stretched away; she seemed to have found a way to live. She was no longer depressed nor even unhappy. She remembered the hard, frozen ground of January and it was another world. Now the summer seemed an eternity, the heat went on and on, the days blazing, the nights mysterious, the moon dilated. It was too hot to do anything, too hot even to lie by the pool with Paula at the club. They closeted themselves in air-conditioned rooms and played tennis in the evenings. The lessons with which Kate now filled her day, flower arrangement, ink painting and tea ceremony, became an effort, and she cancelled them for the month. They would go to the sea, they would go to the mountains Jun said, but could not fulfil his promise for all manner of business reasons.

It seemed the summer was possessed by a race of singing creatures. By the river the frogs chanted and croaked, an elusive bass orchestra filling each night. In trees and grasses crickets and the hysterical cicada worked away in frenzy. She awoke and slept to a noise like interference on a radio, whirring through the heat. The fir trees in the garden were hot and noisy factories of insects, disgorging an endless racket. The bell insect, small and black as watermelon seed, the *kantan* with its metallic twang, the king of the dead, and the demon-*korogi*, the dark insect choir played on.

She learned from Jun that these sounds should not be cursed and thrust away but loved and cultivated, for they were summer's poetry. He told her of the trade and culture and literature of these short-lived singers that went back centuries. He told her of his childhood and how every Japanese youngster deftly hunts his own small choir. He brought a green gauzed insect box and led her to the garden. There they laughed like children and crept about amongst the shrubs in a thickening summer dusk, catching insects in a net until the evening sky was the deep blue of butterflies' wings and their limbs covered with itching bites. The green gauze box was full of scaly, moving bodies, jumping midgets, muscled thighs and a waving artillery of antennas. She held it dubiously as it vibrated in her hands. In the dark garden Jun stood with his head on one side and told her to listen to the songs.

'There,' he said, 'that's the weaver, *ju-i-i-i chon-chon*, like the sound of a shuttle. *Tsuzure-sase, sase*, that's the *kirigirisu*. And the loud one, that's the *korogi*.' His face was serious as a child's.

She began to laugh and could not stop, placed the box upon a rock and put her arms about him. She could not say she had regrets. It seemed love stretched out beyond the flat serenity of the evening, heavy and warm with an inner perfection that overcame all. She was happy. It was enough.

But sometimes, in the hot, still silence of noon when she tried to sleep, she thought again of the child. Its small, dead face came back to her, a weight at the base of her brain in those midday siestas. This summer sleep was no dreamless nap, she slept as if stupefied by a pressure of light and heat. At noon the world lay naked to the sun, stripped of every shadow. A stillness filled the garden beneath the insects' drone. Within it each sound seemed to magnify, the crack of a twig or the papery rustle of bamboo. On the bed she tossed and turned in some twilight region between sleep and consciousness, and the noises broke in her as ugly visions and sudden leaps of heart. Then the child's face floated up within her, its eyes closed, its face stiff and expressionless. She awoke filled with the sickening knock of her pulse, her body covered with sweat. The dream returned each day.

Outside the enormous heat and light pressed on, the garden was drunk with sun. Nothing in it moved. She understood how for some black races noon was the hour of ghosts. It was her hour. At night there was always Jun, and the solid repository of him to deliver her into the present. But even at night, sleep was not entirely bland. In the darkness something seemed to wait for her. She could not explain the nuances of this fear, as she held Jun close, her hands caressing his smooth, neat body. He was the reason for her fears as for her happiness. He was the anchor holding her in this world of exotics and banalities, its sensibilities and barbarities, and its slow consumption of herself. She had begun both to love and to hate the place.

On one August evening they sat eating watermelon upon the raised veranda of their home, with glass and paper doors drawn back. The house though small had a delicate garden of stones and moss and old gnarled firs, costly as antiques. The scents of plants and cooling earth, rose with the dusk.

'Soon,' he said, '*Obon* will be over.'

He explained again how the dead were never far away and once a year returned to earth for several weeks for reunion with the living. Kate remembered the night some days before when she had gone with the family to the cemetery to light the spirits towards home. In the dark graveyard the white globes of the lanterns on graves and the smoke and smell of incense were an eerie sight. But she had clung to the thought that the child was with her in some unseen way, and had known through the month it had been the reason for her restless dreams.

'Soon, the spirits will go back,' he said. 'We light their journey once again with lantern boats launched on rivers and lakes. We will go to Kyoto and launch our own, and see too the great bonfire of *daimonji*.'

On the last day of *Obon* they arrived before dark in the Kyoto suburb of Arashiyama. The town curled in a valley along the Katsura river; already there were crowds. The evening was oppressive and insects were busy in the trees along the river banks; clouds of gnats swarming beneath the branches. The river was spanned by a heavy wooden bridge raised up in ungainly elegance upon a regiment of stilts. People jostled for places on the bridge, leaning over the sides to stare down into the water where a great landing stage had been erected. Crammed upon it was a mass of delicate lanterns, each carrying the name of a departed soul, waiting to be launched.

They went first to the marquees especially erected along the river bank, where for a small sum a priest wrote the name of the deceased on a thin, wooden tablet and placed it in a lantern boat. They requested a lantern for Jun's father and grandparents, and another for the child. But Kate could not let the child's lantern set sail on its lonely journey, jostled anonymously in a ghostly armada. She insisted they take the lantern with them, and launch it on the river themselves.

They crossed the bridge and saw on the upper reach of river small, green-roofed boats punted about. Japanese-style inns lined the banks, each craning its roof behind the other for a partial water view. Their windows, bare and open, were like layers of multiple eyes, each reflecting a different scene. A family ate dinner, a couple dressed in *yukata*, a woman nursed a baby, all oblivious of privacy, all linked within each window by the identical *yukata* provided by the inn. Souvenir shops and small restaurants lined the road. The grey-tiled roofs of the town backed steeply up into the hills behind a temple and pagoda. Everywhere, growing crowds of people, waited for darkness to descend. In the thick, dusty pines the insects resounded fortissimo, the cicadas rattling their last brassy volley of the day.

Boatmen were busy preparing a flotilla of the green-roofed punts for an evening upon the water. Cold dinners of buckwheat noodles were laid on long tables the length of the boats. Beside them stood a row of plaited bamboo cages, each housing a large, black, slim-necked bird. Kate knelt to look. The birds smelled of fish and shifted about uncomfortably in their cramped baskets.

'Cormorants,' Jun explained, 'they use them for fishing at night. We'll see. I've hired us a boat.' She was delighted with the surprise.

But it was still too early. They climbed a hill to a monkey shrine but saw not a single creature. There were only the giant cedars trees full of insect musicians, and a telescope on a viewing platform. Below them the river was like a mirror, fiery now, catching the sunset and dying light, the sky bruised and fading quickly. Soon the boats at the towpath began to fill with guests in summer kimono. Globe lantern lamps were lit by the hundred each side of the river. The lighted interiors of the inns were illuminated on the darkening sky as mysterious worlds of picturesque activity, their flimsy structures like some larger form of glowing paper lantern. Kate drew a breath at the scene below her. It was like a painted tapestry of the past.

Jun aimed the telescope at an opposite hill and through it Kate saw a stream of small figures preparing the fires that would later be lit in the huge form of a *torii*, the entrance to a Shinto shrine.

'There are five great fires lit tonight on the five hills surrounding Kyoto. From here we can see the *torii*, and to the east the biggest of the fires, *daimonji*, laid out in the shape of the Chinese character "*dai*", which is usually translated as "big, but in Buddhism means a "human body". The fires, like the lantern boats guide the visiting spirits back to the other world.' Now on the river the fire had died and darkness thickened beneath the surface. Beyond the valley the peaks of hills rolled away into mist and the night.

'It is time, we must go down to the punts,' Jun told her.

Already the small crafts were pushing out onto the dark river, alight with frail, swaying strings of paper lamps. There was only the night and the reflection now of a world of lights upon the water.

In the punt she set the child's lantern boat carefully beside her on the matted floor.

'It must be launched with the others, while the *sutras* are chanted,' Jun instructed.

Out on the river it seemed they had entered another world. The noise of insects and crowds was far away from their rocking, silent island. There was just the lap of water and the knock of the boatman's pole against the boat. They ate a cold meal laid out for them, of fish, pickles and rice, washed down with beer. As they ate other lantern-lit punts slid past them. Noises drifted faintly across the water. From time to time waterborne shops drew up before them, gaudy with commodities.

The boatmen began to call to each other, manoeuvring the punts into a long line against the staves of a weir, until they were wedged stern to bow like a string. There was the smell of beer and grilled squid and the rich, thick river scent. The cormorant boats swung slowly down before them then, reflective with the blaze of burning logs hanging in a cradle from their bows, drawing the fish to the surface of the water. Flames cut away in the breeze, sparks spitting as the fish swarmed up. Released into the water the cormorants called out in strange, bleak cries, diving for the fish, their long necks collared by metal rings and leads held by the fisherman. As their necks swelled above the rings they were pulled back to the boats to regurgitate the fish.

The fierce glow of the fire passed before them then turned away, the cries of the birds growing fainter. The punts began to break up again, pushing free of the weir and out once more onto the open water. At the same moment on the far side of the river the great armada of sacred lantern boats were being lit and launched one by one, pushed out into the current. The flotilla thickened, the lights bobbing and shivering, moving slowly forward, drawn out into the river upon their journey. Across the silent water came the faint sound of sutras chanted by the priests. The lanterns filled the black road of the river, each small boat bearing its candle and dead identity, jostled together in eerie procession.

'Now,' said Jun, 'now. Put it into the river.'

He bent and lit the small, white candle and the lantern came alive. Kate lifted it carefully over the side, and placed it upon the water. Jun leaned out and gave it a push. It floated slowly away into the dark, a more poignant and solitary sight than anything Kate had ever seen. She put out a hand but the lantern was gone, already drifting away on its lonely path. Other punts had launched lanterns and they too sailed silently behind the child's, pulled on by the dark river's current to their ghostly destinations.

For Jun the moment had already passed, he pointed excitedly into the sky. Far away on the bowl of the night the great shape of the *dai* burst into flames, each part lighted separately, zipping to meet the other until the massive figure glowed, several hundred feet across, astride the far hillside. They watched in silence while it blazed above the town, its red aura lighting the sky and the crest of a slope. As the great *dai* faded the *torii* burst into fiery life upon the dark hill behind them. The lanterns drifted silently on the river beneath the flaming signs upon the hillsides. The child's light was lost to Kate, swallowed up in the dark. She took Jun's hand then and prayed silently for the future and another child.

But the night, spread before her like a picture book of fantasy and curiosity, soon died and would never come again. Months later, she remembered the child's lone lantern floating away across the water, and knew that her life and all it held had ended at that moment. From that day on, Japan showed her another face.

11

Jun stared out of the window, nothing would convince him that he was not right. Only last week he had published an article highly praised for its far-sighted views. Itsuko had given it little attention. From the window Jun stared dully at the dusty roofs of the mill sheds, two girls in overalls walked by beneath the window pushing a trolley of boxes, he felt weary and diminished. Behind him in the conference room they shifted restlessly. Beneath the table Yamamura drummed his feet on the floor, from Itsuko came a small, tight clearing of the throat, and the creak of wood as she fidgeted on her chair. Jun turned again to face them.

'I still say our wage structure must begin to change. It cannot take the strain of continual economic growth. Rising costs and increasing competition will force us to it in the end. Many firms already see this and are changing. We should start now and prepare ourselves.'

'We are a traditional culture, certainly,' Itsuko replied. 'But I see our wage structure as a highly sophisticated industrial relations system. All these Westerners who observe us and criticise pay far too much attention to institutional arrangements without examining functional outcomes. There is no need for any change,' She thrust up her small chin, determined. It was fatal to cross her so openly.

Impatience filled him again. He did not wish, as his mother liked to think, to overturn a whole establishment. He valued the strengths and coherence of their system. Was not the whole world now examining it as some wondrous curiosity. But there were problems no one but an insider could see, that a new age of technology had brought upon them. In the lifetime employment system wages were determined by length of service, age and education, they were not job related. The wage increase followed roughly the thickening shape of a man's life as he moved from bachelorhood to family responsibilities. But old crafts had given way to massive technological change and highly skilled industries. The young unskilled workers were often quicker than older and more highly paid workers to acquire and retain new skills. To use technology efficiently more and more young workers must be assigned to jobs appropriate to their abilities and a shortage of these workers compelled their proper use. And these young men were often of a different mind from their fathers. As Japan changed from a production to a consumer-oriented society they wanted their money now to cash in on the good life that the mass media described. The permanent employment system and the old wage structure did not always sit well with them.

'Our system,' Itsuko said, 'brings the industrial world into line with the rest of Japanese society, where age is highly valued.'

'Maybe he is right,' Yamamura said, 'he is young and can see the future clearer than us. We belong to a different era. Look at the changes we've seen since the war. Probably our industrial structures should also be flexible.' He scratched his head with a nicotine-stained nail. Itsuko turned upon him in displeasure and he fell silent again.

Jun looked at him without interest. He had felt Yamamura's support growing since his return from London, not he knew from any respect for his views, but simply because Yamamura now saw Jun as his future employer, and so found this stand expedient.

Itsuko began to tidy a heap of papers on the table before her. A young girl appeared with a tray of green tea. Itsuko nodded and accepted a bowl, sipping from it daintily. 'We employ a predominantly female labour force, who are paid quite differently. Many are even temporary labour, I can't see any of this applying as yet to us. Your views might be applicable in heavy industries, but the old way is still best for us.

'We employ women predominantly, not exclusively. We have a large male work force too. Why should we lag behind in management practices? In grandfather's day we were known as a most progressive firm, he was one of the first in the industry to institute modern welfare measures.' Jun argued.

Itsuko rested the bowl of tea in the palm of her hand with a small exclamation of impatience. 'Can we not end this fruitless argument?' she said in exasperation. It was not that she did not see things looming on the horizon, a whole army of frightening shadows that threatened her security. Change must come, but gradually. What she feared most was a rupture and diminishment of her authority.

Jun belonged to a new generation, he had no memory of the world before the war, a world that was handed to Itsuko undiluted from the past. The old values were solid as the flesh upon her. She was a pre-war woman brought up in a time when militaristic growth in Japan dominated education. It stressed a pathway of patriotism and self-sacrifice to high ideals. Itsuko still remembered the picture placed in every girls' school during her growing up years. Five pictures of a mother and her son from babyhood to military age, when the mother prayed for his glory as he went to battle and received with grateful tears, the news of his death for the honour of the nation. Such ideals were not easily destroyed, but defeat in the war stained them badly and left the old traditions in limbo. Yet, where other women and lesser men had muddled through, fragmented and disoriented, unable to find a postwar pathway as compelling as the old, Itsuko remained intact. She merely transferred her will from aesthetic and cultural values to the concrete world of the mill.

It was true in her father's time they had been known for progressive management. Her father had instituted all the welfare measures they accepted so easily today. Since her grandfather's time in the Meiji era, the industrial system had never ceased dramatic evolution. Through strikes and rice riots and experimental adaptations it grew, borrowing generously from abroad, rejecting, inventing, improvising, while still cherishing a feudal continuity. It evolved into a wholly indigenous industrial system filled with concepts ancient and modern, peculiar only to Japan. Itsuko took it as a single packet, placed reverentially in her hands. She did not question her role or place nor that of those who worked beneath her. She was part of a system where all things were preordained and the rules excluded rearrangement. What functioned had always functioned and produced all they saw today; she was unwilling to take a young man's risk in directions she considered unnecessary. She stood up and nodded to the two men and turned briskly to the door.

Jun drank down the cooled remains of his tea and followed her despondently, Yamamura hurrying apologetically on his heels. In the office downstairs an exercise break progressed as they walked through. Men in beige overalls and girls in navy smocks swung themselves about. Yamamura stepped forward beside him.

'Your mother is also right, I understand her views. We were brought up together, we are from the same time. But you youngsters have a sharp nose for change.' His voice lacked conviction, his main aim was to ingratiate himself with both his present and his future employer. Jun quickened his pace, and walked towards the shed where they were testing again the air-spinning machine.

As he turned in at the door, the odour of grease and cotton surrounded him. The hum of the new machines filled the shed, it had been working all day. There were no disruptions, it was running well now at the anticipated speed. A row of spindles spun before him, their shapes liquid with speed, the men bowed to him cheerfully from the machine. Sun shone through high windows down upon the spindles, flying like the hundred feet of some great centipede. It was unbearably hot, his overalls stuck to his back, but the discomfort seemed trivial to all that was happening here in this shed. Before him the stream of yarn rushed on, unstoppable now, possessed of its own mad energy.

He made a sign and the machine gave out a tearing groan, and relaxed like a dancer released from an endless pirouette. In metamorphosis it was dull, a heavy bank of metal, obstinate to touch. He brought his hand down and the dance began again, the spindles turning like a chorus line.

To his mother, a machine was a machine, of no more interest than the product it produced, but to Jun, each machine fulfilling its task was as absorbing in character and peculiarities as any group of human statuary. The slow, chewing jaws of the carding machines, lazily turning their rolls of waste cotton, could never be hurried. The quick, slick click of the combers moved in precise regimentation, the threads running from them like gauze rivers, and the bobbins and twisters and cheevers madly winding and spinning, raced like artillery in battle. Jun found excitement and a pulse in this mechanical activity that made it almost human.

He congratulated the men and had established an easy camaraderie with them; they sensed an energy from him quite different from his mother. 'We shall have a celebration and think what we'll turn our talents to next. We can develop this part of ourselves. We can make Nagai famous for its prototypes.' They cheered, then bowed to him and each other.

Jun left the mill separately from Itsuko, who had returned to the Osaka office some time before. He drove straight home, he was early. Usually, when he returned, the house was in shadow, but now an upper window seemed to flame in the setting sun. He let himself in and the house was dim and silent, Kate was not yet back from Paula's. He should have phoned her there, he did not like a lonely homecoming, nobody to greet him, even the maid had gone. This annoyed him suddenly, it was part of the function of a maid to be there to greet the returning. It was only etiquette that a man be welcomed home by the women of the house; Kate was too casual with these formalities.

He went about resentfully, switching on lights in the darkening house, and his annoyance spread. He had not been to Chieko for days; for weeks he had only a few visits. It was not right for him to grow to know the child. His whole relationship with Yukio he had decided, must be reduced to the thin rustle of the bank draft. He could see now this was best, for both himself and the boy. Their lives could flourish then, parallel but not impeded by emotion, the link of blood established but unembroidered. Once the decision was made, he began to try to dampen Chieko's expectations. This was not easy considering her threats, he could not just cut things off, the procedure would be slow and stressful. He must slowly reduce his visits, like an addicted medicine. In the end he hoped he need only face her once in a while. This was what he must work towards.

It was all for Kate, but the anxiety and manoeuvring exhausted him. Her effect upon his life was like the derailment of a train. Because of Kate there was now no ordered sphere for Chieko, her shadow jerked uncomfortably behind him. Had he not married out of context, his life might easily have contained her. Kate and her Western ethics gave Chieko, as a mistress, an importance she did not have in traditional Asian society. He was tired, angry again at Kate's absence, at the closed stuffy house and the need to see about turning on lights and opening windows. Why should he feel such guilt about Chieko, he was doing no more than expected of a man in his position? And however hard he tried, Chieko stayed rooted in his mind and body. He knew he would never be rid of her.

He went upstairs to shower and change into a cool, summer *yukata*. The house was like an oven, full of trapped heat. The carpet Kate had ordered laid everywhere gave off a new smell, he felt suffocated. He tore off his clothes, flinging them down on the floor about him angrily and strode into the bathroom and the shower. When he came down again into the lounge, a last glow of sun surrounded him. He slid back the veranda doors, opening the room to the garden and took a deep breath of the still dusk. A moth settled on the mosquito netting that filled the open window, its wings drumming rhythmically. He poured a whiskey, walking barefooted into the kitchen for ice, swearing that neither Kate nor the maid had emptied the frozen cubes into a larger container, as he liked. He took out the tray and ran it under the hot tap, all the cubes fell out together with a crash into the sink. He swore again, taking them in a bowl back to the lounge to sit down with his drink.

The saw of crickets carved into the silent evening beyond the open windows. In the distance he heard the waterfall, a windbell moved in a tree. He sat on the sofa, resting his feet on the coffee table, restless and depressed, the day repeating on him like stale food. Yamamura's ingratiating ways, and his mother's stubborn thrust of chin seemed to sum up for him all the months since he returned to Japan. His mother's voice rattled through his life like marbles in a can. The tension of it all was unbearable, and putting down his glass, he placed his hands over his ears, as if he could shut out the world. Everywhere he turned he faced an obstacle of some kind, he seemed to live against the grain.

He threw back his drink and stood up to pour another. 'You should not,' Kate had told him before, 'you're drinking too much.' She had put out a hand to restrain him, but nothing else helped him. He sat down again with a fresh whiskey and looked at his watch. In the room the fleshy chairs were awkward to his eyes. It was a delicate Japanese room, matted traditionally, with a *tokonoma*, a raised alcove for art and flowers. Kate had insisted she furnish in a way that was familiar to her. All the weeks spent with Itsuko she told him had destroyed her morale, he was happy to indulge her. The bare, sanded walls had been papered, the natural woods covered with white, shiny paint and the matting with a thick carpet, upon which was placed a recumbent mass of furniture.

In the beginning he had participated willingly in this Westernisation of the house, enjoying its reflection on his cosmopolitan lifestyle so far removed from orthodox ideals. But looking at it now he suddenly felt the objects in the room were like a hoard of bodies crowding in about him. The rich textures and shiny surfaces supported a vertical world. He alone knew the slender nakedness beneath that was the true character of the room. And he saw then that the room, like him, had been changed by Kate to an uncomfortably strange identity. Only the *tokonoma* had defeated her ingenuity, repelling all translation. She left it to its own devices with a scroll and a flower arrangement. It looked into the room like a large sad eye, at the disease distending its fragile body. He raised his glass to its apprehensions, feeling at one with its perplexity. The world thawed slightly with the liquor, he reached again for the bottle.

'You're drinking too much.' He tried to push Kate's voice away. As he stared at the glass in his hand, the door grated in the porch. He waited for Kate to enter the room. She was casual about calling the ritual words of return, he would have a few things to say to her about these matters tonight. He frowned into his glass and shook the ice loudly in annoyance.

It was not Kate but Chieko who stood before him in the doorway. He stared at her in horror. The drink slopped onto his hand as he pulled himself up.

'I told you never to come here.' He took a step forward, Chieko slid past him into the room with an artful twist of her body. Her mouth, red and blatant, in her face, stretched into a defiant smile. He took her roughly by the arm, pushing her to the front door.

'Get out at once. She'll be back soon. I'll come tonight, I promise.' He heard the desperation in his voice. Chieko pulled free of him.

'I've had enough. You can't treat me like this. It's time she knew. I don't care.' She threw back her head, the breath knotting in her throat, as she looked about the room.

'Very nice, very pretty. You don't deny her anything do you? No, you have to do what you're told with foreign women.'

'Please.' Jun looked at the door and then back again at Chieko. It was like a bad dream, he could not believe she stood there before him in his home. She knew what she did by coming here, invading a space where she had no right to be.

Chieko calmly sat down, picked up the glass he had left on the table and raised it to him mockingly. With a smile she tipped back the drink, crossed her legs and wiped her mouth on her hand.

'What does it matter if she knows? Why should she not also suffer? Why should she be protected at my expense? It's all clear to me now. I've been a fool, I did what you wanted, I kept quiet. But you don't care, you hardly come, and the money's not enough. Not enough, do you hear?' She sat forward in the chair like a small, snarling animal. She had already been drinking before she arrived, harvesting courage.

'I want to see her. I shall tell her myself.' She pushed her face up at him. 'I came here yesterday, I watched this house, I saw her. What a pretty wife. But tell me, is she better than me? I know her type. She'll never do the things I do. Will she? Can she?' She pushed herself suddenly against him, her body wheedling. Her breath was sour with drink, and she stirred at that moment nothing in him but a new upsurge of anger.

'Get out. Get away.' He pushed her off him roughly. His mind was full of the emotions Kate would feel if she saw Chieko here.

'I'm not ready to go yet.' She turned back upon him, twisting about him like a mad thing, he could not shake her free. He stumbled backwards into the soft, unresisting sofa as she came down on top of him, her body filled with crazed energy. Her closeness stirred him now, and fear and disgust at what he was feeling only added to his anger. She had no right to confuse like this the careful structure of his life, here within his own home. He flung her away, but she clung to him still, pulling him with her as she rolled to the floor and broke free at last with a laugh. She lay there limply, her breasts heaving in a convulsion of laughter, her mouth wet and open in her face. Her skirt was rucked up about her hips, her legs spread wide. Along the inside of her bare thigh the flesh was white and soft. He stared at her on the floor beside him, the breath choked within his throat. It sickened him to see her there, he must get her out at all costs.

He looked up then to see Kate standing in the doorway.

12

The light was dying on the hill, thickening in the undergrowth to a dense tapestry of leaves. The waterfall rushed down towards the sea against the current of cars struggling homewards up the hill, headlamps burning in the dusk. Kate walked quickly along the steep, road. Far below the lights of the town glittered, the sky was like spilt ink. It was the flat, yellow kindness of Fumi's face she needed like a balm now. Fumi knew Jun better than anyone. Fumi must know who that woman was, what connection she had with Jun. Her limbs moved like a sleepwalker, her mind numbed by shock, until the pictures welled up again, searing through her like a burn. She saw again the woman, spread-eagled on the floor, the white stretch of muscle running up her open thighs. And Jun. There was an empty glass on the table, a smear of lipstick on its rim. There were shoes in the porch, pink strappy sandals with heels thin as ice picks, vulgar and high. And Jun. *Jun.* She screamed his name silently. Horror and helplessness overwhelmed her again. It was a dream. It must be a dream that showed him locked with that woman upon the sofa, his face flushed with drink, his *yukata* loose about his bare body. It was a dream that showed him turning, falling with the woman.

They turned and fell endlessly in Kate's mind, taking too long to hit the floor. Taking too long to fall apart. The shame was hot within her.

She let herself in through the back gate. The garden was quiet, full of shadow and the smell of damp soil and moss. The old house was already captured by night, darkness brooded beneath the eaves and the thick, stunted branches of old trees. The kitchen was deserted, ripe and brown and silent as ever. She could not see Fumi. A soup of fish and vegetables, simmering in a pot, coated the air with sinewy smells. Fumi seemed not about, not in the garden, not in her room. The need for Fumi's kind face grew suddenly tight in Kate, tears of desperation constricted her throat. She went down the hallway, willing Fumi to be in the *tatami* room, busy as always with her crochet, settled on a cushion in the evening light.

Kate opened the door, but it was Itsuko, not Fumi who sat in the room. Itsuko raised her head from the papers she held, a pair of spectacles on her nose.

'What is it? Why are you here?' Itsuko asked.

'I came ... that is ... I am looking for Aunt Fumi ... I ...' Kate could not string the words together.

'Fumi? She went to the doctor. Autumn is here, the evenings are damp, her rheumatism is back.' Itsuko said, her eyes full of enquiry. Kate was silent.

'Can I help? What is it?' Itsuko spoke kindly. 'You're white, you look ill.' She put down her papers, stood up and walked over to Kate.

'What is it? Are you ill?' She repeated again, worried now. Taking Kate's arm she steered her into the room.

'Sit down. Come.'

Itsuko bent and pulled a cushion forward for Kate, then poured some iced wheat tea into a little cup, thrusting it into Kate's hands, before settling herself upon a cushion, waiting. Kate sipped the cold, aromatic tea. It slipped down the hard constriction of her throat, its coldness releasing emotion.

'It's Jun,' she whispered. Against all resolve the words dislodged themselves and Itsuko sat forward alarmed.

'Jun? What's happened? Is he hurt? Is he ill? Tell me at once,' she demanded, remembering his belligerence at the mill earlier that day.

'I came home ... he was there ... with a woman. He was with her ... together ...' Fleshed into words the images grew viciously before her. Itsuko sat back on her heels, the tension in her face relaxed.

'A woman? A woman ...?' she asked, then laughed incredulously with amusement.

'But he is a man, there will always be women.' She offered it genuinely, as comfort, her voice resonant with relief. She had thought there was something really wrong, but it could only be Chieko. Itsuko had known in some way it must happen, sooner or later. For better or worse, it could do no harm to her own plans for Jun, that things were now out in the open. She could understand Kate's devastation.

She had faced her own crisis many years before when her husband set up the geisha, Komayo, in an establishment of her own. There had been countless others after Komayo. It was only the first time that nearly killed Itsuko; after that she learned not to feel.

Any wise woman's pride was her home and her children, she looked no further for fulfilment. But of course, thought Itsuko,

Kate had not that kind of vision. She wondered yet again what Jun had found so fascinating. Itsuko continued to sip her tea. Kate continued to sit in a state of shock before her mother-in-law. The tick of the clock and the clack of the bamboo mortar in the garden marked her pain like metronomes.

'The woman is dangerous, I warned him. I knew she would not stay quiet,' Itsuko offered above her tea.

Her small buffed nails were smooth as petals about a blue flowered cup. The words stung Kate to new numbness. Who was the woman? How did Itsuko know her? She felt she had entered some dark maze of which everyone but she knew the pattern and exit. What was Jun hiding? What life had he had before their marriage? At that moment she knew these were questions held within her since the time they first met. She had been glad not to hear them, glad not to ask. And Jun had offered no information.

'You take it too seriously. She is just, a woman, of no consequence. But I can understand your shock. He should not have had her in the house. Probably she came, unasked. But even so ... not in the home, not in the house,' Itsuko admitted.

She could be kind now, seeing in Kate's shattered face, the means to her own ends. The road ahead already took shape, it did no harm now to offer comfort.

'In Japan, women are used to these things. We overlook them in a good husband. A woman's life is hard, no man can bear what we can. We allow him his pleasures in return for security. If a man meets his responsibilities at home, then a wife must overlook his activities away from it. That is the way it is here,' Itsuko said quietly. Kate looked up in surprise. Itsuko never talked in this tone.

'I have not always been in this position. I was as any other wife while my husband lived. You must not think I do not understand. My husband was like all other men, as was my father and my grandfather. Those other women are of little consequence in the true circle of a man's life. They can in no way challenge the position of a wife.' She spoke kindly, resting her tea bowl on the open palm of her hand before continuing.

'The men in my family were famous as womanisers; their exploits still live on. We do not regard as wrong indulgences of the flesh. We do not share here your sense of wrong. Perhaps that is the difference. We do not see obscenity where you do. I know you see many things in different ways, and this has made your settling here difficult. If you choose to stay here, there are things you must accept. If you cannot, then it is not too late to go back. Divorce here is easy, especially for a man.' Itsuko gave a small, sad shrug, but her eyes slid sideways carefully to Kate's shocked face.

Divorce. The room was nearly dark. A low lamp cast their elongated shadows across the smooth matted floor, like a black substance that flowed out of them. Divorce. The word reverberated in her. How could Itsuko suggest such a thing? Kate drew back with a fear she had not yet felt. The word pulled her together like a slap upon the face. She would never let Itsuko have her way, now she knew her game.

In the silent room, the discharged emotion was solid as granite to Kate. It was not all as Itsuko had said, Kate felt. The ethics she spoke of were remnants of another era, but still alive to her. Jun was so different from his mother, and yet it seemed some residue of the past remained within him too.

Itsuko sipped demurely at her tea, avoiding Kate's eye. What divided them, Kate felt, were not a history of experience, but a whole alphabet of response. Itsuko sipped on, unforgiving as marble, a small noise in the silent room. Kate could not believe it was as Itsuko said. She knew things about Jun his mother did not. Itsuko saw only what she wished. Jun was not callous, nor was he careless. She was sure of everything built between them. There must be a reason. Kate gave a small bow to Itsuko, and walked quickly from the room.

He was waiting almost where she had left him, sprawled on the sofa. The empty glass was gone from the table, the pink sandals from the porch. He scowled in a way she knew hid stricken guilt. Coming back into the room, the shock beat through her again. She could not sit upon the sofa, nor look at the place where the woman had lain upon the floor. She had been ripped into a thousand bits, and yet Jun refused to cope with the situation; he hid behind his scowl. It was up to her, she thought, and became at once calm and managerial.

'I shall get us some coffee, and then we shall talk.' She announced briskly. In the kitchen she found the offensive whiskey glass washed clean of its lipstick mark, draining upside down. She ignored it.

She placed the tray upon a low table on the narrow veranda and drew two cushions to it. The doors were pulled back opening the room to the garden. A few crickets still sang, the night was warm. The moss and old rocks were lit by a garden lamp and took on in the darkness a lunar disguise of cragginess and shadow.

Jun came across reluctantly, flopped down on the cushion and took a sip of the coffee Kate silently served. He did not speak, but looked at her furtively, gauging the route to forgiveness. At last the worst had happened, and in some way he was relieved to share the burden of guilt. Kate appeared calm, as if little had occurred that could not be mended, but this he knew was the British trait of "stiff upper-lip" and could be deceptive. He remembered her face as she had stood in the doorway in that disastrous moment, drained and demolished. He knew to the smallest detail the banality of the scene she had observed. Shame brimmed hotly in him. Their eyes had met briefly before she turned and rushed away. He had slung Chieko out of the house with a force he wished bitterly he had mustered before. For good measure when she struggled, he gave her a blow that cracked her lip as he pushed her through the door. She had stood by the gate, bending to tighten the straps of her shoes, the trickle of blood a dirty weal on her chin.

'Well,' she had shouted across the garden, as he stood angrily in the porch, determined to see her out. 'Well, she knows at last. Let's see how you get out of that.' She gave an ugly laugh and left. The click of her heels vanished at last as she disappeared beyond the gate.

He had straightened the cushions on the sofa, washed the glass and tidied himself. He lit a cigarette, waiting blankly for everything that must now be. Kate had probably returned to Paula's. He wondered if she would ever come back, if his life would ever be the same again. His thoughts seemed detached and unreal, as the event they sprang from. In the dark silent garden nothing stirred. He was drowning slowly in his fate. The dualities of his life had come crashing down upon him like a flimsy house of cards. And he could feel nothing, could not even move, waiting for he knew not what. It was as if he must sit and wait forever, until released by the next event.

It seemed a long time before Kate came back. He was surprised at the change in her. Perhaps she would find a way to make things all right again between them. He did not know what he could do. There would be no way back once she knew the whole truth. Through the open kitchen door he had watched her set the coffee on a tray, frightened by her calm. He was surprised when she took the initiative.

'I do not know what it means, all I saw in this room earlier. But I feel I know you, and I cannot believe there is not a good reason to put his evening behind us. However difficult it is, you must tell me everything. You owe me that much honesty.' Her eyes were grave across the small table.

He cursed Chieko for what she had done, and felt as black and wretched as the small speckled beetle that climbed the window beside them. He forced words into his mouth.

'I didn't ask her here. I didn't know she would come.' It sounded sulky, not how he wanted, he tried again.

'Believe me. I didn't ask her here. She's a terrible woman,' he said fiercely at last.

'Yes.' Kate readily agreed. 'Tell me about her. You must try for both our sakes.' Her voice was calm and even. He nodded, he was anxious to explain now.

'I met her years ago, before I came to England, I met her in a bar. She's a certain kind of woman ... I ... she attracted me.' He sought out the best words. 'I became involved with her. For some years we had a relationship. There was never a question of marriage to a woman of her type. I never loved her. It was physical attraction and a relationship of convenience. Her name is Chieko,' he added, and saw Kate's expression change. He was getting the words all wrong.

It was not what she had expected to hear. She had thought he would protest his innocence.

'I tried to cut it off with her, but she threatened she would tell you if I didn't see her, if I didn't give her money. I did not want you hurt; I did not want her to destroy us.' Any moment now he must tell her the rest, tell her the worst. He searched for the right words but they hung beyond his reach.

'It all began a long time ago, before I met you. Do you think anything like this could have happened after I knew you? Do you think I could look at anybody else in that way? She blackmailed me. And now it has come to this.'

Now he thought, he must tell her the rest. He must tell her of Yukio, now. But she was speaking again.

'It has been a shock. But I'll try to understand. It is something from another life, before we met. I expect I shall get over it.' She gave a wan smile and placed her hand upon Jun's across the table.

'We'll put her behind us. But you must not see her again. Do you promise? If you see her again it will mean all we have between us is nothing to you. Do you promise not to see her? Do you?'

The words he desperately sought to bring forward danced into the distance. The moment had passed, it was too late. To tell her the rest would be too much at one time. He should let her absorb this much first, and later tell her the rest. That would be best, he decided.

'I promise,' he said and meant it.

She could not sleep. Beside her Jun's breathing was even, her forgiveness appeared to release him from further reflection. She however was left distressed and confused. His face was touching as a child's in sleep and showed no wounds or complexities. She wished she could wake him, for the comfort of his arms that might banish her fears. Instead she let him be and lay back, arms folded beneath her head, she was ill with thoughts and fears. There was so much she did not understand. The longer she lived here, the more she knew and the less she comprehended. She had not just to battle with her own jealousy, but to understand a different order of things. Here it seemed a man was allowed many faces to deal with many different situations. Life was parcelled into its separate compartments, each with its own code of behaviour. Here contradictions appeared to her to be the uniformity of life. Jun had tried to explain this to her once long ago.

'We believe a man has two souls. They are not his good impulses fighting his bad impulses, they are his rough and gentle souls. One is not destined for Heaven and the other for Hell. Each is a part of him, each necessary on different occasions. No evil is inherent in man's soul.'

It had seemed exotic to her then, a strange plumed bird of thought. Now she faced the reality of it all. Life was like a mortgage from a bank, everything must be paid back, everything was borrowed, man was a debtor, and accounts must be kept of words and deeds and gifts. It was a complex world to be walked through warily.

Tears of rage choked suddenly in her throat, sweeping away the numbness of earlier shock. She wanted to wake and shake Jun. Instead she got up and left the room. Downstairs in the dark kitchen she drank a glass of water. The room was silent, a clock ticked somewhere. Then the tears began, rising in her, a great wave of passion that carried her away.

Jun came quickly downstairs, and found her locked into hysteria, wet with tears. He picked her up and carried her back upstairs, kissing her neck and murmuring contrition, desire already stirring within him. She lay beneath him exhausted, and wept again at his touch. Then she folded him within her arms and slept, before he could stir her to life.

13

Paula was deadheading the roses in her small angular garden. Her house, on a prestigious stretch of hill along Kitano-cho, was high above the centre of the town. The area was densely populated, houses clung precipitously to the hillside, traversed by narrow uneven lanes above a panoramic view of the town and bay. Paula's house was an awkward, perpendicular affair crowned by a turret, like a holiday hat. It fitted no known school of architecture but appeared assembled in whimsy. Far below them in the distance, the town of Kobe spread in a long, narrow ribbon, hemmed in between the sea on one side, and the hills on the other. Osaka could be seen in the distance from Paula's turret, a mass of concrete and gasometers glinting in the sun.

It was peaceful in the garden. Paula snipped carefully between thorns. Behind her a marmalade kitten played in the undergrowth, jumping suddenly from a hydrangea bush. The bell at its neck sounded in the warm, clear morning.

'Thank God,' said Paula, 'all that humidity has gone. I love the autumn. You must see the maples, they're almost garish they're so splendid. The trouble with you Kate is, you're caught between a past and a future.'

The kitten pranced sideways at Kate's feet upon its long, thin legs, cuffing its paw at a toffee wrapping James had dropped the day before.

'Whatever do you mean?' she asked.

'Well,' said Paula, 'everything is changing here. The old mores have given way to more flexible forms, families are nuclear, no longer communal, marriage is mostly by choice and not arrangement, old people live on their own. Women are asserting themselves in new ways; everything is moving and widening. Jun knows that, he's part of today's world, but he's not yet able to free himself from the past. But he will, his marrying you is proof of it.' Paula sat back on her heels to gather up a pile of dead and shrivelled rose heads.

'Jun's telling you the truth, it's something from his past,' Paula reached out to snip absently at a dead leaf. The kitten jumped to it as it fell.

'I'm all right.' Kate gave a small smile and then a cry, as the kitten jumped from a bush to land on her shoulder. She extracted him gently and placed him on the path again, laughing now with Paula.

'He's James's,' Paula announced. 'We thought it would do him good. He's better lately, I think we're through the worst. There's another American family returned here whom we knew before. Their son Tom was James's friend, so you can imagine the difference that's made to things. It's great to see him happy again. And that's what you need too, some friends. I don't mean like me, or all those other women I've introduced you to in the foreign community. None of us can understand your problems. You need someone in your own position, in a mixed marriage whom you can relate to. I'm sure it would help to know someone like that. I want to introduce you to Mandy Takeyama. I met her on a train and got talking to her, I think she's also lonely. I told her about you. She's English too. She wants to meet you. I'll ring right now and see if she's in.'

Mandy Takeyama had straw-coloured hair cut in a close arc about her round face, clear light eyes and open pores upon her chin. She lived in an unfashionable part of town, on the second floor of a *danchi*, an apartment block. Stone stairs led up to a narrow alley that traversed the centre of the block, and where all the front doors looked like back doors, of scrubbed, unpainted wood. Beside each protruded a mechanism to heat the traditional tub in a bathroom just inside the front door. From kitchen windows hung umbrella-like clothes lines strung with bits of washing. On the railing of the stairway quilts were draped to air in the morning sun. The alley between the rows of front doors was crowded with tricycles and small children. Mothers chatted with one another at open doors. A chained puppy snapped at Kate and Paula's heels.

Mandy's door was open, she called to them to come in. The porch was so narrow they stood one behind the other to take off their shoes. At one side of the entrance Mandy's brogues stood neatly beside her husband's, a size larger than his and crushed down at the backs. She came forward and knelt at the *genkan* and reaching for her husband's shoes, thrust them into a cupboard, to make room for their own in the small entrance.

'My husband's away for a few days. In Japan when the man of the house is away, they usually leave his shoes in the porch, so his absence is not apparent.' She laughed in a good natured way, greeting them as they stepped up into the house.

It was the tiniest living space Kate had yet seen, a single room of six *tatami* mats, with a small kitchen and bathroom off it. It was bare and neat. Mandy lived Japanese style; the bed of quilts stored in a deep cupboard during the day, a low table and cushions brought out in exchange. Some hanging plants and shelves of books, a television and a small low chest were all the furniture in the room. A large chart of the acupuncture points on the human body was pinned upon a wall. The kitchen appeared spotless beyond a beaded curtain that clicked and swung as Mandy pushed through it with a jug of coffee. She knelt, and poured gracefully into earthenware mugs.

Kate gazed about as she sipped the sweet creamy coffee. The room, though small, seemed spacious, a Zen scroll hung in the *tokonoma* alcove above three flowers in a vase. Mandy offered little Japanese sugar cakes and a variety of wafers. Her husband, she told them, worked with Kobe Steel as a research engineer, and she was studying acupuncture and moxibustion. She had met her husband in Japan, when she came to learn about martial arts. Her interest in acupuncture began when she was cured of an injured knee. The philosophy underlying it intrigued her.

'An imbalance in the meridian flow is what creates disease,' she told Kate; her eyes direct and uncomfortably assessing. Kate felt her critical judgment in spite of Mandy's smile. Mandy pointed to the acupuncture chart on the wall. 'All those positions on the body are *tsubo*, where the energy flow can be struck by inserting the needles, or applying heat, as in moxibustion, when a small piece of the mugwort plant, called *mokusa*, is burnt.' Her face was round and flat, almost Japanese; Kate began to wonder if she had some Japanese blood in her, a grandmother maybe. She had found recently she was unsure of her assessment of people. Many foreigners now looked nearly Japanese, and the Japanese all looked as if they might have mixed blood, the distinguishing points seemed suddenly vague. Kate looked again at Mandy's straw-coloured hair and pale eyes and decided she must be losing her grip.

'The whole philosophy of oriental medicine is based on the theory of *ying* and *yang* and on the Five Element Theory, made up of *moku*, wood, *ka*, fire, *do*, earth, *gon*, metal, and *sui*, water,' Mandy continued. '*Ying* and *yang* are not negative and positive forces, but complementary. Take the stomach for instance, the outside is *yang* and the inside is *ying*, and the head and feet have a *ying-yang* relationship. And each of the five elements generates another. Wood burns, creating fire. Fire turns wood to ash, ash becomes metal and metal can melt to liquid. They oppose each other too. Water destroys fire. Fire destroys metal. Metal destroys wood and wood stops soil, soil blocks water. So, if you have trouble in the kidneys it can be because of the liver, lungs or spleen.' Mandy spoke authoritatively, offering another wafer.

All this, it further appeared, along with physiology, pathology, oriental philosophy and Western medicine, Mandy studied in the Japanese language at an institute for oriental medicine in Osaka. She had been just over four years in Japan.

'All that in Japanese?' Kate asked astounded and alarmed. 'I'm not bad at the language and I knew a lot before I got here, as far as conversation goes. But I doubt if I could manage all that in four years,' she admitted.

'Oh well, where there's a will there's a way,' Mandy shrugged casually.

Kate shrank back and wondered what thick walls within herself prevented a more fluent understanding of Japanese. She listened to Paula question Mandy on her adaptation to Japanese life. She did not seem lonely or perplexed, as Paula had explained.

'I love it here. I can't say I ever had many difficulties in adaptation.' said Mandy with a smile. Kate began to hate her smooth, round face.

'I found only help and kindness,' Mandy continued. 'In the beginning of course, things were strange, but the secret is not to fight it, but to go with it, to be Japanese. And I did just that. I learned a different way of living and one I think far superior and sensible to ours, far more perceptive to economy, hygiene and bodily needs. And I found everyone accepted me, everyone was kind.'

As Kate remained silent Paula asked about Mandy's Japanese parents-in-law.

'They're farmers,' she said, 'in Shikoku. We go back there at *Obon* and New Year. Last year we helped them harvest the rice. Sometimes they come and stay with us. For a while in the beginning we lived with them. I loved it, I fitted in easily, they seemed happy with me. Of course, I tried my best to be a Japanese daughter-in-law. I did everything I could to please Kenji's mother. I got up early, I cleaned the house, I cooked when she taught me, I massaged her shoulders, I massaged her legs. I went last in the bath, I made them all up their lunch boxes before they went out in the mornings. I forgot I was not a Japanese. I'm very fond of them all, although I'm not saying it wasn't a relief to come and live alone with Kenji, and do something for my mind.' Mandy laughed and turned to question Kate on the circumstances of her life.

Kate thought, as she had many times before, how different things would have been had Fumi been Jun's mother, instead of Itsuko. And she too, thought Kate, might also be able to please a good-natured farmer's wife. The differences that divide existences cannot be judged by the sum of things. Her circumstances were different from Mandy's, it was impossible to compare. And the more she thought the more she was sure, Mandy would not have put up with a fraction of the things that made Kate's life. She would have stamped her sensible brown-brogued foot, and stomped out of that Japanese life. Kate had the feeling she had been summed up in Mandy's clear eyes, as weak-willed and self-indulgent. Kate tried to explain something of her life to Mandy, but none of it sounded right.

Mandy listened to Kate and then shook her head.

'You live in a different world. And as you see, we're too poor for Kenji to get into any trouble,' she said in reply to Kate's bitter reference to the philandering of Japanese men.

'Sometimes, Kenji stops off for a coffee or a quick drink with a friend on the way home, once in a while he goes out with the boys. Kenji's not an expense account man, he's not at that level. None of his friends have enough money either to get very far. I'm glad for him to have a good time. Our dire financial straits always keep him in order. All this bar-going in Japan, it's just harmless drinking for most of them, you know. I haven't met any of your problems here, or I've slipped through them if I have,' Mandy declared.

Soon she looked at her watch and found with relief they could go. Mandy told her to come again whenever she wanted. 'But ring me before, because I'm usually at the institute, this morning you were lucky. And my advice to you is; get yourself moving. Get going, get a job. Interpret or teach English. Even a jackass can teach English here and make a living from it. It's what everyone does.

'And listen, if you can't swim with the current, strike out against it. If you'll excuse the observation, you're standing still and drowning. Get off your ass. I can see you're unhappy. Strike out. If you're strong enough, you'll swim,' she said briskly, then shut the door.

They should never have come, thought Paula as they turned away. Kate's face was tense with unspoken strain. All she had thought was that they were both married to Japanese, and that common ground would help Kate. It had been foolish of her not to realise that such different circumstances of marriage might offer little relevancy. The visit had probably done more harm than good.

Kate walked ahead of Paula, quickly down the stairs. The sun had gone behind a cloud, shadows consumed her coldly. She swallowed hard as Paula's steps caught up with, her, sympathetic and supportive; Paula understood. But if she was fair, Kate knew Mandy was right, at least in the last analysis. She *was* standing still, and she *was* drowning, in some slow and nameless way. She must strike out against the current. The cliché stuck in her mind, offering a banal comfort. She did not think she would see Mandy again; there was little to connect them. There must be a way to turn negative into positive. If Many had done it so could she, Kate thought. She must put that woman Chieko behind her, she could do nothing to them now. Kate turned then and smiled at Paula, determination in her eyes. The sun came out and lit again the bright quilts upon the wall.

14

The meeting with Mandy upset her. She did not go home after leaving Paula but walked aimlessly, absorbed in her own emotions. She did not know where she walked, furrowed deep within herself. The sky threatened rain, and it was late afternoon. To Kate life seemed suddenly full of alternatives but few choices. She was the sum of her own limitations. She looked up to meet the painted peacock eyes of a mannequin in the window of a store, and found in the blatant gaze a familiar audacity. It was the face of the woman Chieko again, and she turned away quickly.

'Kate.'

Someone tapped her on the shoulder, and she turned to find Yoko beside her. Her lazy, feline smile, uncritical as ever, filled Kate with a rush of warmth.

'It's been so long,' Yoko smiled. 'Don't say you're in a hurry. We'll have a coffee.'

Kate nodded in pleasure. It was weeks since Kate had last seen her. Yoko's visits to the family were rare, the lines she must not overstep and the frequency dictated was a silent code of etiquette understood only by her and Itsuko. Her life after all was one of digression, and she had chosen it herself. She had made her own bed and now she must lie on it, Itsuko unfailingly implied. The laxity of will that was Yoko's road in life must in no way reflect the family honour. Itsuko was firm, relenting only on occasion. But Kate liked Yoko, liked the ease of her, so different from her sister, and above all liked the slatternly instincts that made her defy conventions. She thought her brave and bold. She had told Jun so, but he only shrugged. A woman of her class, he said, should not do those kinds of things. He spoke as narrowly as an old woman, and she fell silent in surprise.

Yoko's voice was low and husky, thick as blotting paper. Awareness seeped from her like a scent. Her eyes saw little further than her appetites, and since these were satisfied she could be generous, and uncritical. Kate marvelled at these differences in her more liberal-minded in-law as they walked along together. Yoko pointed out a coffee shop and they crossed the road towards it. Pushing open the door they entered a pseudo-Tyrolean world, of cuckoo clocks and yodelling music. They found a table and Yoko ordered Vienna Coffee without prior consultation.

'It's the best thing here,' she explained regally. 'You must have it. This place advertises that it makes the best coffee in Kobe.' Her eyes, bold and amused, held Kate's in unhurried scrutiny.

'Tell me how you've been, away from the main house and my sister's short, tight rein?' she demanded, raising her eyebrows and lowering her voice, deepening their intimacy.

'I'm fine,' Kate replied mechanically, trying not to remember the past few days.

'Oh she's a difficult woman, my sister. I'm not disloyal, I'm just stating a fact. I can understand what she's put you through, I've had my own collisions with her, and I'm just a sister, not a daughter-in-law.' Yoko chuckled to herself.

Kate realised, sitting with Yoko, that it was the first time they had met alone, in all the months Kate had been in Japan. Each time she had seen Yoko before had been with the rest of the family. Looking at her now she thought how different and yet how great was her resemblance to Itsuko. With no more than a slight inverted twist, Kate could imagine Itsuko a greater sensualist than Yoko. For she was just as much a creature of instinct, at the mercy of her sensual nature. Finding no outlet this energy petrified in Itsuko, but the power that filled her was that same dark secret force that moved Yoko along her dissolute way. The coldness Itsuko showed her sister was not only harsh convention, but also vindictive jealousy at Yoko's promiscuous ways.

All this Kate sensed, as she watched Yoko chat about trivial things. And she felt the same envy stir within her that she knew must stir in Itsuko, or in any woman caught and held within herself by social rigidity. She looked down into her coffee cup, at the thick sweet lid of cream and knew she must find some way to hang onto her sanity, and a wider view of things.

'I've always admired you. You're brave, to live as you do, divorced and with a career,' Kate said, wishing to develop the bond between them.

'I'm not like my sisters, they're pre-war women. In the old days a woman belonged like a piece of baggage to the family she had married into, even her children were not her own possessions but could be taken away by a mother-in-law. I don't find it hard being a divorcee. I can tell you it's better to have been married and divorced here, than never to have married. If you've married people know there is nothing wrong with you. If you've never married they presume it's because of physical or mental faults. I'm happy. I have friends, I have my work, I travel. I enjoy myself.' She smiled and shrugged, sipping contemplatively at her coffee. Taking out a cigarette, Yoko lit it with a small gold lighter.

'You know, I admire your independent ideas. Don't take any notice of Itsuko, you come from a different world. I know,' Yoko laughed.

It seemed to Kate that she and Yoko had changed places. Yoko had escaped her mould, while Kate lay trapped within it.

'I'm sorry,' Yoko said suddenly, licking cream off her upper lip. 'I'm sorry things are so difficult for you at this moment. Itsuko told me on the phone. It's a pity Jun didn't rid himself of Chieko before he met you. We hoped she'd keep quiet. I expect it's a shock. Chieko is from the past, you must realise that. I'm sure he wouldn't look at her now. But it's a difficult situation for you. The child complicates things so much. I can't understand how Jun allowed himself to be trapped like that. Some women will stoop to any trick. She was the wrong type to get involved with.'

Kate held the creamy coffee on her tongue and felt it turn thick and sour. She lowered the cup slowly to the saucer.

'I don't understand. What ... what child?' She managed to ask. Yoko clapped a hand to her mouth.

'Didn't you know? Didn't you know about the child?' She demanded in embarrassment. Kate shook her head.

In the room the buzz of conversation sounded suddenly unreal. Everything seemed to have stopped in Kate as it had at the moment she saw Chieko. Yoko was speaking again but Kate hardly caught her words.

'... well it's best then, best you should know. I'm glad it came out. You should talk to her. Have it out. I would. She lives near here, Jun rents a place for her, I often pass it. I'll show you.'

It had rained while they were in the coffee shop, the roads were wet. Yoko produced an umbrella. They walked through the arcade of fashionable shops in Sentagai, busy shoppers and passed under a railway track and the thunder of trains. Kate walked as if drugged, she felt so tired she wished to lie down there on the pavement and sleep, and never wake up again.

'There.' Yoko pointed to an apartment house, hemmed in between a hairdresser's and a bookshop. 'The fourth floor, those windows there. He pays a lot of rent. This is a fashionable area.'

Kate stared up at the fourth floor windows, as if in a dream.

'Oh Look, there they are,' Yoko said pointing across the road.

Chieko rounded a corner, and crossed the road. A child of three or four walked beside her dressed in brown shorts and a pale blue school smock, a green handkerchief pinned to his collar. A yellow satchel bumped upon his back. He walked along, talking earnestly to Chieko under the umbrella she held above them both, stopping sometimes to hump the satchel higher on his shoulders. His knees were knobbly and his ears large like Jun's. But for the rest the child seemed all Chieko. Yoko pulled Kate into the narrow entrance of the bookshop as Chieko and the child walked towards them and then disappeared into the block of flats.

'Lets go,' Yoko said, pushing Kate forward. 'Shall I come home with you? You've had a shock. I'll get a taxi.' She hailed a passing vehicle that drew up beside them.

'I'm all right. Don't worry.' Kate insisted, shutting the car door firmly upon Yoko. As the taxi pushed forward Kate turned to the window and saw Yoko close her umbrella. The rain had stopped.

15

She could not bear to go straight home, but walked down to the little shrine beside the waterfall a distance before their house. The autumn dusk held a touch of death and dampness. Japan lived closely with its spirits, and these she felt about her now in the trees and in the weathered wood of the old shrine. In the courtyard stone lanterns stood amongst ginkgo trees, stone lion-dogs guarded the shrine, and in the distance the sound of the waterfall cascaded heavily after a night of rain. The murmur of the water washed through her, reminding her of how long she had listened to its constant whispering. Now she was so used to it she hardly heard it.

There was no more anger; there was nothing in her now but tiredness. Returning to the house she pulled back the sliding doors of the lounge, opening the room to the garden. Darkness thickened in the trees, the sky had faded to a bluish light. Lamps came on in the neighbour's house, a church bell sounded from the town, there was the smell of fish being fried. Rocks and stone lanterns in the garden absorbed the shadows and grew mysterious. No natural spontaneous growth was allowed.

In a Japanese garden; there was never a large shady tree to sit beneath, as there had been in the gardens of her childhood. Here, beautiful though they were, gardens were for observation, not participation. Trees were not allowed to grow in an unrestrained way. They were cut and pruned and chopped about, discipline was applied to them each year of their sprouting life, until they no longer ignored authority but conformed to a short and powerful shape, where all energy was held within strong and obedient forms. It all followed the Confucian philosophy of devotion to duty. Such discipline was seen as the road to spiritual growth, as in the physical disciplines of Zen, or in the arts, or human relationships.

In the dusk the sky had became a deep luminous blue, as it folded to the night. Dogs began to bark, a moth fluttered in. Soon the glass of the window reflected only her own face and the light in the room behind. She felt she understood nothing any more, and closed her eyes, waiting for Jun.

'Kate,' he had said, laughing. *Laughing.* 'Kate, what's wrong?' He took her by the wrist and pulled her against him. 'What is it now? I thought it was over, understood. We talked last night.' The words came out of her then.

'There's a child, isn't there? I've seen him.' The words echoed through her.

He released her, stepping back. The room became very still, the silence flowing between them.

'Tell me about this child. Don't you see that you must tell me? I don't understand you.'

'I didn't know how to tell you. I hoped you need never know.' The words sounded hollow and inadequate. There was no way to predict now what she might do.

'Don't you see that you should have told me before, in the beginning, before we married?'

'I was afraid you would not marry me.' He could not find the words he wanted, words to calm, words to obliterate, words to diffuse the truth. There was no way to avoid now the ugliness of the situation. In the face of truth there was nothing he could say.

'But don't you *see* what you've done? If you had only told me before there was a chance we could have found a way. Oh don't you *see*, don't you *see*?'

He remembered her hysteria the other night and became frightened for her now. But she did not resist when he placed his hands upon her and pushed her down gently into a chair. He opened a cupboard and poured neat whiskey into a glass and steered it to her lips, then sat beside her, rolling his own glass back and forth between his palms.

'Kate ...'

'Don't you see,' she began again. 'Our relationship is a lie, and has always been with this secret behind you. Everything I thought we had, has in fact never been.' She spat out the words and he hung his head, unable to look at her.

'I'm sorry. I'm sorry.' The phrase fell foolishly from him.

'Kate ...'

She took no notice as she packed a bag, not daring to look, knowing his pleading might even now draw her back to him

'I cannot stay, I must be alone, I must think. I'm so tired and confused. I shall only be at the Baileys', so there is no need for you to worry. But don't try to come there, to bring me back. I must think, You must give me time.'

She looked back once from the gate and saw him standing in the doorway, silent with the guilt and shame of it all. She willed herself to shut the latch and turned quickly down the hill, looking for a taxi.

16

In the Baileys' home the sumo wrestlers faced her from the wall, the familiar candlestick lamp and the *kai-oki* box with its thick, green tassels sat squarely on the table as before. Only she was changed. Paula put a hand to her mouth to hide her shock when Kate explained that her life was wrecked.

'Oh,' she said. 'Oh.'

Pete stood silently beside his wife and shook his head in disbelief.

'It's something that happened in the past that I have to learn to live with. But I just cannot find a way,' Kate said despairingly.

'Of course you can't,' Paula murmured.

'You can stay here as long as you want, you know that,' Pete told her in a low voice.

'Yes, I know, that's why I came. Who else could I have gone to? I'm just sorry to place this upon you both,' Kate replied conscious t of how her personal void involve them.

Paula moved closer and put a comforting arm about her. In his usual rational way, Pete sought as ever to be fair. He could not believe the worst of Jun, he liked him as a man.

'I'm sure Jun faces a terrible dilemma in himself. I can understand why he couldn't face telling you.'

'He should have been honest,' Kate said fiercely, the words knotting in her throat.

'There's no excuse for him.' Paula drew herself up in defence of Kate.

Soon they stopped the pointless discussion and let her go to bed. It was as if she was physically ill, too weak to remove her clothes. And when she lay down, the sleep she thought would overwhelm her did not come. There was a sudden breeze outside and the sound of rain again upon the glass. The room was dark, from downstairs came the ring of the telephone and sounds of Pete and Paula moving about. Beside the bed the luminous hands of a clock moved smoothly through the night.

'I did not want it to happen like this. I never wanted to hurt her.' Jun's voice was hollow on the phone as he spoke to Pete. 'I was trapped. I didn't know how to tell her. It was like another life; how can I expect her to understand? I just hoped she would never know. Is she all right?

'Whatever she decides, you must give her time,' Pete advised.

The days spiralled in tight about Jun. Wherever he looked he was thrown back upon himself. It was the waiting that was hardest, alone, locked into a disaster of his own making, he told no-one, least of all his mother. He hoped within a few days Kate would return, then he stretched the days to a week. And the worst was that within all this a need for Chieko filled him in a shocking rebuttal of sombre facts. He was torn with the need for both women, for different things within each one. His desire for Chieko could melt his bones. Yet, when he contemplated the choice to be made there was not the slightest question. There was nothing more he wanted than Kate, nothing he wanted to regain more than her love and respect. He did not see Chieko, she did not ring him.

It was Fumi who first came to know. She worried quietly at her crochet and worried at the stove above the steam of piquant soup or apples in a pan. Kate was not there. Fumi had phoned and phoned, and paced about the garden of Jun's house, peering through windows into dark interiors. At first she thought Kate was out and busy, but with each day her fear grew, as did her intuition before a wall of silence. Nobody said anything, but there was an edge of energy in her sister that Fumi had observed before at times of malicious satisfaction, or the completion of some inner puzzle. It was something felt, as faint as that, but she knew her sister well. And Jun when she saw him or questioned him, sank into silence. There were tensions, she could feel them, dark and brooding. It was soon apparent what was amiss. The daily help, taking a wrongly delivered letter down to the main house, confided in Hirata-*san* the maid, who confided in Itsuko and Fumi the next day.

'I hear,' said Itsuko coldly, 'that she has left. Is this so? Answer me.'

She confronted Jun in the morning soon after he entered the house, to pick her up on the way to the office. She stood with her back to the window and the morning sun spread behind her like an aura. Beyond the veranda the garden filled the window. He felt as he had that dark night long ago when, on the edge of the moonlit garden, he had looked up at her in contrition, nine years old and shivering. 'You are a Nagai, the eyes of the world are upon you.' Her words came back to him again, words she had placed upon him as tightly as a skin. He hardly dared look at her now.

'It is not her going that is wrong, but its manner and its timing. If we had sent her away it was one thing. That she has deserted like this is another. What will people say? She must be brought back at once and then later we can send her home, send her away. That will be different.' Itsuko said angrily.

'I cannot just bring her back, like that. There is no way she will come but of her own accord. It is all my fault.' Jun argued in distress.

'Fault? How is it your fault, except that you should have been more careful. It is too late to be concerned with fault, we must think about results. People will talk, what will it look like, what will they say? If your wife cannot live here, then that cannot be helped. *Shikata ga nai.* But I will not have her shame us like this.'

The light caught her unflatteringly and Jun saw at last that she was old and tired and intractable; she was caught in her own charade. It enclosed them both now, inescapably.

'I'll try,' he promised, unconvinced.

'There is another thing,' she said harshly, picking up her briefcase. 'I have had a phone call from the plant. Last night there was a break-in. They were after the blueprints of the new machine. The night watchman disturbed the thieves and they dropped the file as they fled. Whether they took any pictures, I cannot say.'

Jun took a step forward in alarm. 'Tamura. It can only be Tamura.'

'I told you he had not given up. We must be extra careful until that patent is through. But he didn't get away with it.' Itsuko gave a triumphant snort.

'We must go straight to the mill. The police are waiting there for us.'

Jun nodded and followed her out, his thoughts divided and confused.

Kate did not know if she was more afraid of the doors that had shut around her, or the space that lay beyond. She was safe with the Baileys, and from the window of their Kitano-cho home, watched a world of colour and sound and life. Only she it seemed, was dead in a world of the living. She needed to sleep, and when she woke to the brilliant mornings, she needed to sleep again.

She tried to read the books on Paula's shelves, but everything between the pages seemed to apply to her state in life. Everything seemed written by people who understood. The finding of this poetic understanding was more painful than the understanding normal people gave with their wholesome clichés. There were times when she could not bear Paula's voice, bouncing along with careful inflexions of sympathy. She wanted to scream, but instead returned to her room. The days past slowly, she lost track of how many. She was here alone to think things out, but her mind would not move.

'It has been almost two weeks. What can we do to help her? I've been thinking, Steve Lever in the office, who's in charge of the heavy industries section, has a couple of clients arriving from Spain who can't speak a word of English. He's looking for an interpreter. The job is only for a few days, but will probably lead to others. I thought Kate could do it. It might put some life back into her, break the vicious circle of depression.' Pete looked inquiringly at Paula, as she rummaged thoughtfully in a bag of wool for a ball of orange thread.

'I hope we can persuade her.' She squinted up at the light, threading a strand through a needle.

Kate sat in the garden with James's kitten, a frail ball of fluff. It leapt suddenly from her lap to a windblown leaf, leaving her nothing but its vanished warmth. She stared at the empty cup of her hands. She could not sit around at the Baileys forever but could see no way to a future life.

Paula carried a tray of coffee over to where Kate sat in the garden. The breeze rustled through bamboos. The musical chimes of the waste paper truck passed by in the road outside, soliciting magazines, newsprint and boxes. Paula stirred the sugar in her cup and spoke her thoughts immediately. She explained about the job, and was surprised at the ease with which Kate accepted the idea.

'It will get you out of this depression and help you pull yourself together. It will be for the best,' Paula announced assuringly.

17

Steve Lever was small and rodent like, with pinched features. He had a tendency to tell flat jokes. The talk and translation was technical, Kate had often to consult a dictionary for unfamiliar terms. The Spaniards, Carlos and Alberto, were middle-aged men. Carlos was bald as a darning egg, Alberto's large eyes looked out at the world from some private despair. She knew she was critical of them, but her interest in the job was half-hearted. They called her competent, but after the first day she was exhausted.

She had tried every excuse to save herself from accompanying them that evening, too depressed to cope with a night on the town, with strident bar-hopping, constant drinking and an obligation to translate the thoughts of other people. But they pressed her kindly, and Carlos presented her with a bottle of French cologne. They left her no way in which to refuse the farewell evening.

She had never been to Namba, the busy night quarter of Osaka, except as a transient tourist, whisked through by Jun in broad sunlight on an initial city tour. She hardly remembered the place beyond a density of bars, dubious facilities and the occasional pimp. She had seen only its noon-time face and was unprepared for the licentious reality. In a dressing of neon lights, dark buildings were consumed by brilliance, like a forest of tawdry Christmas trees decorated for the night. Narrow pedestrian lanes traversed bars, cabarets, clubs and massage parlours, all peddling erotic wares. The bars were thick as weeds about them, their slim entrances wedged between more extrovert institutions. Some bars were stacked like the cells of a honeycomb in multi-storeyed buildings, or burrowed beneath the concrete world into hidden basement caves that throbbed with music, drunken men and the slop of whiskey glasses. Steve Lever knew his terrain well. After a meal of steak, cooked and cut and eaten with chopsticks from a griddle, he steered them to a variety of places to sample the high and the low of the area.

Steve Lever took his friends first to the cheaper bars where the women wore strong perfume and had harshly-dyed ginger hair. They found a seedy cabaret with an asexual striptease, whose girls were thin as winter branches and pranced about like drum majorettes. The Spaniards were intrigued by a karaoke bar, where sad customers sang sad songs off key to a simulated beat.

They soon left the karaoke bar and passed an establishment where naked women wrestled in a ring of mud, and a coffee shop where waitresses wore no more than fish net stockings beneath a frilly apron. They found a bar where the women were dressed in saris, and another that appeared housed with nuns. As they walked the warren of streets Steve pointed out the "love hotels", whose baroque exteriors and gaudy lights occupied every other Japanese street corner. Here, rooms hired by the hour were filled with fantasy interiors, strange auto-erotic devices and closed circuit videos of hard core porn. Every worthwhile Japanese company, Steve nodded knowingly, kept accounts at cabarets, bars and the better class of these hotels, to entertain clients and visitors. In this way Japanese business appeared openly to collaborate with the underworld, who ran and owned this cosmos of the night. The Spaniards suggested a quick massage. Kate felt by Steve's adroit evasion of that request, that she was the deterrent to their pleasures. They looked at her in relief when she announced she would leave them after the next bar. Steve pushed open a small, dark door and they followed him inside.

'This is a high class place. They know me here, you have to be careful in Japan, you can't go to places you don't know, you can be ripped off for a hundred dollars a drink.'

The bar was spacious and quiet after the loud and garish road. A grand piano was played softly in a corner by a young man in a dinner jacket, the place was low-lighted, the walls hung with antiquated mirrors flecked in gold. Two or three women at once came forward to greet them, guiding them to a table. These girls were different from those who inhabited the cheaper bars, they were quieter and well-mannered, their clothing expensive, their grooming perfect. The very sight of them depressed Kate; in her present frame of mind, this was the worst place she could have come to. The image of Chieko was everywhere. It was in just such a place that Jun had met the woman.

The hostesses made no effort to include Kate in the group. They fawned over the men, lighting their cigarettes, feeding them titbits, placing cheese-straws between their lips with kittenish giggles. Both Steve and the Spaniards were reasonably drunk and easily diverted. Their primitive inclinations required no translation to the women, and Kate leaned back in relief. Ignored and forgotten in a libidinous world, Kate not ungrateful for the moment. This subculture was like a nightmare she had suddenly stumbled into, and all she wanted to do was leave.

A woman next to Steve, in a blue velvet dress slit to the waist, leaned forward and stroked his knee. He sat back with his arm resting along the back of her chair and raised his glass for another drink. The Spaniards were similarly involved with the women clustered around them. Kate observed the women resignedly as they sipped discreetly on their beers, skilled in the emotional manipulation of men through the practise of centuries. This world of nightlife was an escape from the rigid world of the day, the other side of the Japanese social coin. It was just after nine o'clock as Kate prepared to make her apologies and leave. The night began and ended early in Osaka. Most of the Namba opened at five and closed at eleven. Kate anticipated no trouble getting home. She would take a taxi to the station, and return by train to Kobe. As she stood up a loud voice across the room drew everyone's attention. A short, corpulent man entered the bar. His coarse grey hair sprang up in abundance and was parted just off-centre. He was greeted by the madame of the bar, and joined by several hostesses. His importance overrode the watery notes of the grand piano.

'It's Tamura,' said Steve standing up in surprise to hail him. They met and bowed on neutral ground in the middle of the room. Steve returned to the table followed by Tamura and a further entourage of women.

Tamura stood back in an offhand way, shaking hands with the Spaniards. To Kate he gave only a brief bow, but his eyes rested on her in a manner she did not like. When he sat down she found he had placed himself beside her. He leaned forward, ignoring the hostess beside him, to bring out with difficulty some words of English that sounded like an unknown tongue. He was visibly relieved when Kate replied in Japanese, producing politely predictable questions. While she talked his deeply hooded eyes roved her face before he turned away to banter with the other women. Then, with Steve he touched on some area of business and a light argument started. He had some connection with Steve's firm and had met him through these dealings.

'A grasshopper. You will have a grasshopper.' Tamura turned back again to Kate. She did not understand why he was talking about grasshoppers, and tried to refuse the offer.

'I must go. I was about to when you arrived,' she protested.

'It's a drink,' Steve reassured. 'He'll be offended if you go now. There's no hurry, wait a bit.'

Kate sat back again in the chair, imprisoned by etiquette.

The drink arrived, bright green and frothy in a shallow glass. Kate's head was already electric with drinks, she had not wanted another. Tamura leaned forward and touched the small glass.

'Drink,' he ordered and waited for her verdict. Her mouth was filled by a minty sap, she nodded polite agreement, replacing her glass on the table.

'Japanese women all like grasshopper,' Tamura announced, jerking his head at the bar hostesses, who appeared to Kate like a many-hued species of identical bird sipping in unison on their bright drinks, cooing and flirting, as in some complex mating dance.

'It's nice,' said Kate, seeking a way to leave, waiting for Tamura to turn away. Instead he moved forward in his chair, his belly girthed by a brown snake belt, his crotch pulled tight and bulbous. His interest appeared to deepen.

'Your name, tell me again. I didn't hear. Why are you here in Japan? Are you married? Who is your husband? He's not one of these men? No? Why isn't he here? What does he do? You want a job? You want to work for me?' He pressed his questions like ammunition and Kate drew back as if attacked.

She gave him her name. The fact that her husband was Japanese seemed to excite and unsettle him. She explained about the interpreting job, which led to more facts about her, and he listened attentively.

'You're too beautiful for such jobs,' he told her, insinuation written on his face.

She sipped again at the grasshopper, feeling unexpectedly grateful for his attention. The evening at the bar, and the days behind, had left her feeling an aberration. Tamura wanted to know about her husband, but became silent as she told him the little that she wished. Drawing away, he eyed her strangely.

'I know your husband.' Tamura announced, and Kate could not hide surprise.

Tamura stared at her, his expression unfathomable. She decided he looked like a hog.

Tamura chose his words carefully, speaking with respect. He explained he had once worked for Jun's father but now had a business of his own. He knew them all, Itsuko, Yoko, Fumi and Jun. He had been invited to the centenary party earlier in the year. He inquired adroitly about the welfare of the family. He told her the fears of a seven-year-old Jun before a new machine on a visit to the factory many years before.

'Well,' said Steve when he heard the connection. 'It's a small world.' He returned to the blue velvet woman and another in grey who had appeared to his right.

Kate stood up to say goodbye, and with her last words translated for Steve further plans for the night to the Spaniards.

'I too am going to Kobe. I am leaving now as well. I have a car and a chauffeur, I can take you back.' Tamura stood up suddenly and bowed. Kate hesitated.

'That's great of you Tamura-*san*,' Steve accepted for her, relieved to transfer his responsibility. Kate nodded reluctantly, it might be alright, everybody knew him, Steve, Jun, Itsuko. There could be no harm with these references, in spite of her apprehension. She was tired and did not look forward to the cold, metallic chug back home on a train filled with late night drunks. She bowed her thanks to Tamura, then followed him out.

As soon as they stepped out of the bar, Tamura's car slid forward, large and black and imported, filling the narrow road. Kate climbed gratefully inside. The chauffeur shut the doors and also closed a glass partition separating himself from Kate and Tamura. The car moved forward, gathering speed and the locks clicked shut automatically. Kate turned to Tamura.

'Jun is away in Tokyo, on business. I'm staying with friends in Kitano-cho until he returns. I'd like you to drop me there,' she explained.

Tamura nodded silently, his eyes upon her. She did not like the way he sat in the middle of the seat, close up against her, not as he should by the window. This left little room to stretch her legs. The car moved on through densely lit, narrow streets. At times there were signs and façades she recognised, the red neon moon of a massive Turkish bath she had passed earlier that evening, a river, a bridge, a street of gaudy, paper maples.

Soon they nosed into the main road and began to speed forward. Beyond the window the dark density of Osaka was unfamiliar, and she could make no sense of their position or direction. She began to feel uneasy, Tamura did not speak. In the closed and isolated cell of the car, alone with him, Kate was aware of the man in a new way, and drew back against the door as far as she could. Tamura leaned forward, pulling back the glass that separated the chauffeur from them. In the low, rough voice of Osaka slang, he issued some orders to the man, then shut him off again. Kate did not understand the dialect, her ignorance of what was said added to her nervousness. Tamura changed position, moving nearer. Kate caught the odour of liquor and bad teeth. She drew her legs in further and wished she had gone by train.

Tamura watched her growing fear with pleasing exhilaration. He could not believe his luck. Just when he had thought it was all up with the Nagais' and he must accept his fate, when he had racked his brains and Sakamoto's and everything had failed, he was presented with this gift. There was no way now the Nagai family could possibly escape him. He would pay them back at last for every slur they had cast upon him. Everything he had wanted would soon be his, they would come crawling to him now. He coughed to suppress a chuckle. In the meantime he could allow himself the liberty of some pleasure.

Reaching out, he settled his hand upon Kate's knee. She felt the pressure of his fingers kneading into her bone, and panic and repulsion filled her. Pushed into a corner of the seat by his heavy body, she was unable to avoid him, and he laughed as she tried to push him away. On her knee his hand moved firmly to force her legs apart. She tried to wriggle from under him, hitting out, calling for help to the chauffeur, but the man registered nothing of the scene behind him.

'He is used to my little ways,' Tamura chuckled, gripping her hand. A thin, linked bracelet on her wrist broke and fell to the floor as she tried to pull away. Outside faces and façades came forward then disappeared. Nobody could help her. In the distance she saw a traffic light, red and far away. She willed it to remain.

The car slowed and stopped at the light. She brought her knee up, hard and at an angle to catch him in the crotch. Tamura groaned and doubled up. Kate unlocked the heavy door and pushed it open, almost falling from the car as the light turned green. A truck braked suddenly as she ran across the road, weaving between on-coming vehicles. From behind her came Tamura's voice, swearing loudly, calling her back. She looked over her shoulder and caught sight of his face at the car window. She began to run.

Her thought was to dodge him, then find a taxi back to Kobe, it would be too late now for a train by the time she reached the station. She set off along a dark street, her breath throbbing in her as she ran, her footsteps pounding emptily, Namba's unhealthy glitter already lost and far away.

18

She chose the narrowest, darkest alleys but the car like a great malevolent bird manoeuvred them all, pursuing her. Unable to gather speed, the car followed her, grazing walls and plastic dustbins standing in the road. The streets emptied suddenly into a wide thoroughfare. Kate paused in fear and confusion. She could not see a taxi to hail, and she could not stop to wait. Tamura's car was approaching again. To escape she must keep running. Panic pushed her into the road again, and the oncoming cars hooted angrily. More dark streets lay ahead of her, and she plunged into them. The fronts of small shops were shuttered and dingy, rolled metal doors concealed what appeared to be workshops and garages. Few people were about, Tamura's car was behind her again, and she knew she had been sighted.

The breath tore at her lungs; she did not know how long she could keep running. The streets closed in upon her, her arm grazed a wall, her head swam, there was nowhere to hide. The drone of the car grew louder, bearing down upon her. Looking up she saw she stood beneath a railway bridge and it was not Tamura's car, but a train that thundered overhead. Its caterpillar of carriages lurched and rumbled against the sky, lighted windows filled by the faces of commuters.

Behind her she heard a sound and turned to see Tamura's car had stopped a short distance away. The chauffeur was already out of the car and Tamura was opening the door. She ran on again, her heart thumping.

The street opened suddenly into a wider road, well-lighted and with some parked cars, a few people stood about. There were several ornate 'love' hotels, whose familiar lurid flourish Kate almost welcomed now. In between these buildings were small residences with open, lighted porchways. A half-curtain covered in Japanese fashion each door, a row of slippers waited invitingly. In several of the houses elderly women sat in the porch. One old crone was wrapped about the knees in a red chequered blanket, and Kate rushed towards her.

Tamura bruised his shin on the heavy car door in his haste to get out and follow Kate. After a few steps he stopped and looked about; he had not realised where they were. Watching Kate duck beneath the curtain of the house across the road, he could not believe his luck. If he played his cards right he held an ace in his hands. He grinned and turned and re-entered his car, directing the chauffeur's attention to the house. The man laughed as they drove away.

'Please,' Kate said. 'Please.' The breath caught in her throat, her mouth was dry with fear.

The old woman smiled, her deep-set eyes dark as watermelon seeds. She folded up the red-checked blanket and stood up.

'Please.' Kate put out a hand and touched the woman's sleeve. The old crone smiled again, revealing a few sparse teeth. Slipping her feet out of her wooden clogs, she stepped up into the house.

'Come,' she ordered. 'This way, please.'

Kate looked back over her shoulder, she could not believe Tamura was gone, She turned and followed the woman along a narrow corridor filled with the odour of drains and damp rotting wood. The old woman showed her into a small, matted room and motioned her to sit.

'I'll bring some tea,' she said with a show of concern and Kate smiled gratefully. The woman stepped back into the corridor, leaving the door half open. Kate leaned back against the wall and looked about the room. It was small and bare but for the table before which she sat, and a bed of quilts, a fluorescent light illuminated the room with a thin, mean glow.

A loud male voice sounded suddenly from below. Within a few moments a young woman passed by the open door and clattered down the stairs. Kate heard her greet the visitor, who followed her back up the stairs, passing Kate's open door. The old crone appeared again, all smiles above a tray of tea that she placed upon the table. Kate drank the warm green liquid, but could not eat the biscuits the woman pushed before her.

'I feel better now, I just need a taxi back to Kobe.'

'Rest a little, I've called someone who can help you,' the woman said, regarding Kate silently, her dark melon-seed eyes small and shifty.

Kate heard another arrival in the porch and a male voice shout out again. Peering round the open door, the old woman shouted down in answer. Then, bowing to Kate, she hurried out again. Kate listened to the discussion at the door, then heard the old woman call up the stairs. Soon another young woman appeared, and again brought the visitor back up the stairs, passing the room in which Kate sat. Kate realised with growing apprehension that she must be in some kind of cheap hotel or even worse, a brothel. The smell of drains pressed heavily upon her. All she wanted to do was leave.

'Thank you I feel better. I'll get a taxi home now,' she told the old woman who now reappeared, followed by two men.

One had a crew cut, the other permed hair, one wore a black suit and the other a shirt of a shiny material. Kate recognised them as gangsters, and wondered if Tamura had sent them. The men sat down at the table with her. They smiled, showing mouths with gold teeth.

'I'll bring some tea. The old woman hurried out again,

Kate was left alone with the men. From upstairs came the sound of an argument and then a sudden laugh. The men regarded Kate silently. The one in a black suit lit a cigarette and spat from his lip a speck of tobacco.

'You want work?' asked the one in a gaudy shirt. 'You want money?' He undressed her with his eyes.

'I was lost, someone was following me. It's all right now. All I need is a taxi home,' Kate said firmly. She wondered if there was a chance of running from the room.

'You could earn good money. There are many opportunities for a foreign woman in the bars,' the one in a white suit told her, leaning across the table.

Kate noticed that his nails were coated with clear varnish and neatly manicured, like a woman.

'What kind of work? I might be interested. I need the money.' She made the words sound as innocent as she could, a plan forming in her head. The one in the bright shirt laughed and nodded.

'Of course you need the money. We can show you where it is.' He exchanged a vulgar laugh with the black suit next to him.

The old woman returned with bottles of beer, and filled two glasses for the men.

'How good would the money be?' Kate asked.

'That would all depend on you,' the white suit laughed into his glass. 'We'll take you to someone who can tell you more.'

'Then I'd better smarten up,' Kate stood up, and asked the old woman the way to the bathroom.

Kate stopped as if to adjust a slipper as they stepped beyond the room. The old woman turned left along the corridor, but Kate stepped to the right and fled. In a single movement she seemed to reach the porch, and push her feet into her waiting shoes. She was in the road once more. From the house she heard a roar of anger and began to run again, the men following behind her. She had a slight headstart, but nothing more.

She was back again in the dark narrow alleys, crowded with rows of tiny, huddled houses. Behind her the insistent beat of feet closed in. A stone underfoot threw her almost off balance. The silhouette of houses pressed against the sky and seemed to swing wildly about her as she ran; a sudden, bright window slashed the blackness. There seemed no way to end this night. She felt like a rat in a laboratory maze, and the fear of capture seized her.

There was another wide road before her, traversed by a level crossing. The lighted entrance to a subway appeared, but she rejected that and ran on. She found herself in the lighted tunnel of a deserted shopping arcade, windows shuttered by metal blinds. Advertisements for yogurt, cosmetics and pornographic films flashed from walls and billboards as she ran. In the arcade a few elderly women stood about, and they called to her and to any passing men. The rhythm of feet drew nearer. A small house, shuttered for the night was before her and Kate crouched down behind some potted bushes beside the door. The men came level with the gate, and passed it, running on. As last there was silence. She waited until it seemed to be safe, and then stood up, setting off in the direction she had just come, crossing the arcade into the darkness of the opposite side. She prayed for a main road and a taxi to release her from the nightmare. It seemed she had fallen into another dimension from which there was no way out. She watched the moon blankly as it sailed on its way high above her. She did not know where she was.

Three men stood before a small fire at the side of the road beneath a low bridge. They looked up as she came level with them. The light of the flames shredded their faces, throwing shadows about their eyes. One had matted hair and wore a long ragged overcoat, another was bald and the third pulled a woollen cap low over his brow. All three wore footwear common amongst Japanese labourers, a long canvas sock with a black rubber sole and divided toes, and resembled the cloven hooves of animals. Breathless and terrified, Kate was unsure for a moment if she faced men, or Satyrs.

One of the men called out and began to walk towards her. His eyes were in shadow beneath his woollen hat. She wanted to run and could not, standing petrified before him. Then blackness welled up within her again.

19

Jun watched his mother unfold the letter and push it across her desk to him.

'Read it,' said Itsuko hoarsely, her face old as antique china. The letter lay on the glass-topped desk, dominating the room. Itsuko seemed to recede behind it, beyond her files and telephones and the waiting day. They had barely arrived in Osaka, hardly settled at their respective desks in adjoining office rooms, before she summoned him. Her voice on the interphone had been so faint he came at once, he thought she was ill.

'Read it,' she commanded again.

He looked first at the end. It was signed by Tamura.

> It was the greatest pleasure last night in Osaka, to meet for the first time at the club, Golden Dream, your beautiful daughter-in-law. We spoke for some time, and I was able to observe what an intelligent and charming woman you have bestowed your illustrious name on. I explained my acquaintance with your family, and at the end of the evening, wishing to offer what assistance I could to the daughter-in-law of an old friend, inquired if I could provide the convenience of my car for her journey back to Kobe. She told me your

son was in Tokyo, and she was staying with friends during his absence. She accepted my offer, but after a short distance asked to be set down. Surprised as I was, I complied with her wish. We were at this point near an undesirable area of Osaka and I was concerned. Your daughter-in-law is a foreigner, new to Japan and innocent. I felt sure she did not know of the notoriety of this particular part of Osaka. I followed her in my car at a distance, until I could be sure she was safely on her way. I was troubled to find that she seemed deliberately to enter that disreputable quarter, Kamagasaki, and moreover there in the Tobita area, an establishment of ill repute, a house of prostitution. My mind refuses to wonder at her purpose there, and it grieves me to be the one to convey this information to you. But my obligation as an old friend, forces me to overcome my hesitation. This information is of importance to you.

The old and illustrious name of Nagai makes your family particularly vulnerable. I would not like this information to get into the hands of any of our more spurious magazines, whose aim is only to spread the vicious practice of slander and character defamation. My concern is that this information be kept only to ourselves, and that these consequences be avoided. A foreigner, in an area like that, can easily be traced. To this end you can be sure I have sworn my chauffeur, who witnessed with me all I have described, to absolute silence. He will keep his word as a loyal retainer. As for myself, you can put all trust in my discretion.

I continue this letter with a request, but I am sure you will at once see the pertinent connection with the above matter. Both our companies have been involved recently in the development of a certain new mechanical process. Your knowledge and development is in advance of my own, and I have for some time considered approaching you for a form of direct collaboration. This seems to me to be a convenient moment. A sharing of your knowledge would facilitate a quicker termination of my own project.

In view of the first matter discussed in this letter, I suggest an immediate delivery of your blueprints would be in your best interests. I am not an unreasonable man and am prepared to wait forty-eight hours before I shall be forced to consider taking certain regrettable steps. I enclose herein a trinket left by your daughter-in-law in my car. Perhaps it will help to verify all that is stated here.

Jun could not look up, but kept his eyes on the letter. The shock beat through him, embroidering rapidly in his mind strange scenes and disjointed fragments that refused to fit together. His mouth was dry, he could make no sense of things. It must be a lie. How could Kate have met Tamura? He lifted his eyes to the desk upon which Itsuko now laid a thin, linked chain. He stared at it in distress. There was no doubt it was Kate's, he had given it to her himself. Kate knew little of Osaka, and nothing of the notoriety of the area called Kamagasaki. He went over the letter again, trying to read between the lines. On the desk the bracelet was closed at the clasp and broken along the chain, as if it had been ripped from Kate's wrist. There must have been good reason she wished to leave Tamura's car. She did not know him as they did, he had told her he was a friend. Jun looked up at Itsuko in agitation. She appeared to have shrivelled within herself.

'She's in danger, she's in trouble. God knows what has already happened to her, what Tamura might have done.' He stepped forward urgently, his mind dissolved by fear for Kate. He knew the club mentioned by Tamura. How was Kate there and with Tamura?

Behind her desk Itsuko stirred, blood flowed back into her face. She saw a future that waited now like a door to receive her exit. She clenched her fist in exasperation. Their honour was in jeopardy and all Jun still thought of was Kate, whose fate was inconsequential, compared to the destiny of the Nagais and all they stood to lose.

'Do you not see what she may do to us, the position she has put us in?' Itsuko rasped across her desk.

He understood the blackmail, he understood the horror that must fill his mother's mind. But what seized him now before all else, was simply the thought of Kate. Perhaps it was proof of how much he had changed, proof of his own confusions, that he could not give more than a passing thought to the fears that filled his mother's mind. She thought first, beyond the loss of life or even her blueprints, to the loss of family honour that slander, real or false, would bring. As close as the throb of her blood, was the duty to their name. To Itsuko the shame of notoriety was more unthinkable than death. She clenched her fist again. She would not be defeated by that upstart, Tamura.

'I must go and find her. It's the only way,' Jun decided.

'I must go,' he repeated desperately.

'No,' Itsuko ordered, she sat forward in her chair; the word creaked about her. In the glass of the desk and the blade of a paper knife Jun observed her reflection.

'What are you thinking of? How can you go? Think clearly and beyond your emotions. If Tamura has had the audacity to be this bold, you can be sure he will let no movement of ours slip through his fingers. Tamura's connections reach beyond ours, that gangster Sakamoto is his brother-in-law. Who knows what spies they have around, you would be followed. Then who knows what more they might have to load against us or misconstrue if you were seen in that area. No person of repute sets foot in there. I forbid it,' Itsuko drummed her fingers imperiously on the desk.

She was right, factual as usual, crafty as an animal, protected by detachment at a moment of danger.

'Then we must go to the police.' He argued heatedly, pictures of Kate, too terrible to translate, filling his mind. 'We do not know what might have happened to her, I cannot sit here and do nothing, her life may be in danger. I must find her. Only the police can help.' His voice broke in desperation. 'I'll phone now. I'll phone.' He stepped towards the desk, but Itsuko half-stood as he reached for the receiver and held his arm, her hand determined and reproachful.

'What are you thinking of? Have you lost all rationality? To go to the police would be to make the whole thing public. We do not know what your wife has done, what the situation is, nor even where she is exactly. We know nothing except that our own position appears most vulnerable. To go to the police at this stage is to lay everything in the open. Who knows then where it may go.'

'But we cannot sit here like this and do nothing!' Jun's voice rose, Itsuko cautioned him to speak quietly, she glanced nervously at the door.

'Who said we shall do nothing? Do you think I am not concerned for you, for me, for your foolish wife, for our name? I will not accept this intimidation by Tamura, how dare he. I intend to hire private detectives. There is a firm we have sometimes dealt with for routine office matters, for checking the backgrounds of personnel. They are discreet and thorough. I will phone them at once. Tamura will not have his way,' Itsuko announced, her anger thin and sharp.

She reached for her telephone book, then dialled the number of the detective company, but it was engaged. As they waited to try again, a secretary announced a visitor for Jun and he reluctantly turned to go.

'I'll let you know when I get through. Take hold of yourself. Keep calm,' Itsuko advised.

His visitor was from an insurance company, an appointment arranged some days before and soon over. Jun leaned back in his chair alone in his room, filled with agitation. Light fell through the open slats of the blind shading a brilliant sun, and lay in bars across a corner of his desk. The room was still and quiet and looked out through a glass window into the activity of the outer office. There was movement, he saw the luminous patterning of data information on a computer screen, a girl with a tray moved slowly between the rows of desks handing out green tea. He stood up and paced about, jumping to the phone as it rang.

'They are coming within half-an-hour,' Itsuko told him, her voice precise and in control again. Jun nodded and replaced the receiver.

He sat down again and tried to convince himself that a solution was near, but nothing helped. He stared ahead of him into the office, thoughts running wildly through his head. Kate. There was nothing he would not give for her safety and return. He reached again for the phone, he must speak to Pete, the Baileys would have been the last people to have seen her. Before he could make the call, Pete himself phoned.

'Is Kate with you?' he asked.

'I had my hand on the phone to ring you,' Jun said.

'We're worried,' Pete explained briefly about Kate's depression and the job with Steve Lever that they had hoped would help.

'She rang in the afternoon and told Paula she was going with Steve and these Spaniards to Osaka for the evening. We were glad, we thought it would do her good. But she didn't come back, it got late and we were worried. I phoned Steve, he was already back home and said Kate left well before him with a man called Tamura, who said he knew you. He was to drop Kate back in Kobe. Then, not long afterwards, we got a call from Kate. She sounded strange, she wouldn't talk or say where she was, except that she was all right and she would not be back. She sounded confused, just kept repeating she was all right and that we shouldn't worry. Then she rang off abruptly. I can't tell you how we felt. But then we thought maybe she was back with you, we were sure of it. We thought that would explain her emotional state, and that she didn't want to tell us. But if she's not with you, where the hell is she?'

'Have you heard of a place called Kamagasaki?' Jun asked.

'It's an area or dropouts or untouchables or something, isn't it?' Pete said. 'A place no one wants to speak about.'

Jun began to explain from the beginning of that morning, his side of the story and Tamura's threat. He explained about the area Kate was trapped in, the kind of place it was.

'Private detectives will take too long. I cannot wait. I must go myself, without my mother knowing. I shall find her,' Jun said, suddenly filled with decision. He could not expect Pete to understand Itsuko's labyrinthine reasoning. But it seemed he did, for he at once agreed with her.

'She's right,' Pete said. 'You should not go there at this moment, whatever you feel. Who knows what Tamura has in mind, what move he might be waiting for you to make. You cannot take the risk if this place is as you say. Where would you start? How could you go from whorehouse to whorehouse asking for your wife. God, its unthinkable, you're open to anything then. No you can't go, but I could. I could go without any kind of risk.'

'You?' Jun asked, hope spreading through him.

'It's the only way.' Pete's mind was clear. 'I'll find her, if she's there.'

Jun's replaced the receiver slowly on the hook, filled with relief and sudden hope. Occasionally in the outer office faces looked up, glanced briefly at him and then returned to their work. The truth of his need for Kate was now clear. He rested his forehead in his hands and wished that experience was not so bitterly bequeathed.

20

'I do not see,' said Sakamoto 'how this can any longer concern me. I deal in success not in bungling. My reputation is at stake, whatever our relationship. If it is known I am connected with you and your inability to do a job, people will laugh. Sakamoto is not laughed at.' He scratched his crotch below a red silk smoking jacket.

He had not wanted to see Tamura. He had bigger things on hand than this trifling feud between his brother-in-law and the Nagais. Every few days Tamura turned up to discuss some hare-brained plan or beg advice, almost paranoid about his tiresome spinning machine. It was of no interest to Sakamoto, it was not his line of things.

'I gave you some men. They could have got those blueprints for you, had you planned the operation with more precision. I have done what I can, this is your affair, it is not of interest to me. Some things you must do yourself.' Sakamoto was firm.

Sakamoto's favourite Alsatian dog, five years dead, was stuffed and sat beside him still, glass eyes faithful and unmoving. Sakamoto placed an ashtray on its head and knocked a cigar against it. Tamura was an embarrassment.

'But I have the woman now, I have this evidence, they will give me what I want.' Tamura boasted.

'But you do not have the woman. She escaped. If you had controlled yourself, if you had thought more clearly and not have aroused her fear, we would have her before us now. That might have been interesting.' Sakamoto shrugged.

He wished Tamura would go. Any moment now the leaders of a rival gang would arrive for discussions on the collaborated expansion of illegal operations in Hawaii and the States. Japan was too small for Sakamoto, it was now an age of internationalism. Japanese mobsters must not lag behind in the thrust the rest of the country was making into international markets. Time was getting on, he signalled to some henchmen engrossed at a *mahjong* table. Tamura saw his appointment was over.

'Even without the woman, I have other evidence in my hands. I saw where she went. I can prove it. That will be enough. I have written to them already. They will have no choice but to give me what I want,' Tamura said again.

'I don't want to hear any more. I am not interested. It's your affair. I have visitors coming.' Sakamoto waved him away impatiently.

Tamura stood up reluctantly, ineffectual as always before Sakamoto. With battalions of minions to promote his criminal practices, Sakamoto seldom failed. He was king in a world of his choosing, not an outcast like Tamura knocking on the door of the mercantile aristocracy and hereditary wealth. It was easy for Sakamoto. Tamura turned disconsolately to the door. On the stairs he was forced to step aside for the passage of dubious dignitaries and a swarm of black-suited henchmen. They passed and Tamura continued on his way, unsure as always of his worth in the house of his brother-in-law. Wherever he looked in life, he seemed always reflected as a very small star on the periphery of brilliant constellations.

21

Much earlier Kate woke, and lay in the bed, watching the first glimmer of steel light brim into day. Then she closed her eyes again and slept. The warm bed was her only reality, like a raft in an unknown sea. All she remembered was that she was safe. Now the sun exposed the room about her, the bare hardboard walls and a blue tiled sink in a corner. A bulb hung naked on its wire, a calendar with scenes from *Noh* was pinned to the door. She wondered where she was.

She sat up in the narrow bed, and found she was still dressed. Someone had removed her shoes and a pair of slippers waited by the bed. Kate sat up and slowly swung her legs out of bed, and pushed her feet into the waiting slippers. At the sink she saw a new paper wrapped soap, and a fresh towel had been placed over a rail. She washed her face and combed her hair. A metal desk stood under the window and shelves in the room were crammed with yellowing papers and a pile of labelled files.

The sound of voices pulled her to the window. She looked down from an upper storey into a narrow road. A row of dilapidated houses was brightened by a weak sun. The tiled façade of a bathhouse occupied part of the road, and a dirty apartment block, in which all the windows had been blanked out, carried the sign "Hotel". Before an open-fronted garage some assorted junk lay about. A queue of men, who appeared to be vagrants, did nothing to alleviate Kate anxiety about where she was. Strange flashes of memory returned to her from the night before, and were gone before she could pin them down. Outside the room was a steep ladder-like stair and Kate climbed down carefully. At the bottom of the stairs bundles of string-bound blankets and old clothes stood about. There were two doors on her left, she chose one and pushed it open.

A plump, balding man wearing heavy spectacles and a white open necked shirt looked up from where he sat at a table. Several other men sat about the table with him, but they did not appear to be as young or as energetic as the balding man.

'You're awake. Do you feel better?' the man asked, pushing back his chair and standing up. Kate touched the square of sticking plaster at her temple, nodding in affirmation. He walked over to where a kettle sat steaming upon an oil stove and made a cup of coffee.

'There, come and sit down and drink that. Sugar?' He put in two spoons and stirred it, placing the mug in her hands. 'We can get something to eat if you want?' She shook her head at the thought of food, but drank the coffee gratefully.

'I'm sorry,' she said, 'but I can't remember' your name.' 'Father Ota,' he replied. 'Today we have our post to prepare.'

He indicated a mound of envelopes and printed matter piled upon the table.

'Twice a year we send out a report on this area. Do you remember much of last night?' He sat down and slipped a folded sheet into an envelope and reached for another.

'Where am I?' Kate asked, the coffee mug warm between her palms. The room held the smell of its cheap hardboard walls and fumes of the oil stove.

'This is Kamagasaki,' Father Ota told her. 'Have you not heard of Kamagasaki?' Kate shook her head.

'Literally translated "Kamagaskai" means "Rice Pan Point",' Father Ota explained. 'Some time ago the government tried to change its name, they called it "Airin Chiku", "The Town of Neighbourly Love". But no-one calls it that, it's still "Kamagasaki". You can't change reality simply by changing a name.'

An old man beside Kate nodded in agreement as Father Ota sealed shut another envelope

'And this building we're in,' Father Ota continued, 'We call this, "The House of Hope".'

Behind thick glasses, his eyes were kindly and observant. There was a gentleness about him that encouraged Kate's trust; his smile was quiet and tranquil. Around the table the other three men were elderly, their skin weathered and creased like hide.

Kate remembered then the faces of the men around the fire the night before. She remembered their split-toed footwear, like black hooves. She did not recall them carrying her here. It had been Father Ota's face she saw, concerned and bending over her when she opened her eyes. The men had stood in a huddle to one side of him, and she had started up when she saw them.

'It's all right.' Father Ota had placed a hand on her shoulder, pushing her gently back in a chair.

'You're safe, this is a Christian Mission. The men are harmless, only poor. They carried you here when you passed out, they didn't know what to do with you.'

He spoke in good English. She stared at the men, trying to remember, then the one of them stepped forward, and asked politely if she was now all right. In his rough hands he held a woollen knitted hat that she remembered him wearing the night before. Kate nodded, but turning again to Father Ota, she knew, whatever the night had held, he was a man she could trust.

He asked no questions. Thinking of it now, she found it strange, that he had accepted her arrival so easily. He had dressed the cut on her temple, shown her the room upstairs, and placed clean sheets on his own bed; where he had slept she did not know, for she knew no more until this morning. Now as she drank the coffee, her mind was still numb.

'Don't you want to go home?' Father Ota reached out for another envelope from the pile on the table. She stared at him for a moment, and looked down into the coffee cup, confused.

'Or you could stay here a little longer of course, if you want to.' He looked at the top of Kate's head, bowed despondently above the mug.

'Thank you,' she said, sinking back into silence.

This makeshift room with its smells of paper, wood and dirty old clothes seemed suddenly preferable to the home she must eventually return to. She suddenly remembered that she had phoned Paula the night before, when she regained consciousness. There seemed no need to phone again this morning, for what did it matter, they had heard from her, they knew she was safe. She let the thought slip from her mind, grateful to be free of obligation. Nobody knew where she was. Even she herself was not yet clear about that. But she was safe, in some unknown place that neither offered anything nor asked of her.

'This doesn't look like anywhere I've seen before,' Kate responded at last.

'It isn't,' Father Ota replied. He repeated what Kate had said in Japanese to the other men, around the table, and they looked at her and laughed in a good natured way.

'Where did you learn your English?' she asked Father Ota.

'In the United States with our Mission,' he replied. 'I was there several years. I have been once to England too. I can tell from your accent you're from there. Have you never heard of Kamagasaki?' Kate shook her head again.

'Few foreigners have,' Father Ota continued. 'We're a well-kept secret, or a kind of open secret if you like, even to the Japanese. It's not polite to know about us. We exist without existence.'

'I don't understand,' Kate said, bewildered.

'Come.' Father Ota beckoned and stood up.

He led her through a short corridor, past the stairs she had come down, and the bundles of clothes. He opened another door into a large room filled with men. They queued in a docile file, before a pair of massive pots, whose appetising smell warmed the room. The men shuffled slowly forward, a line of ragged dejected looking men whose age was indeterminable. The food was ladled out by a couple of younger men, and two helpers whose work appeared to be weeding trouble-makers from the queue. Loud arguments erupted at times before the cauldrons, whose steam rose to opaque the spectacles of the man behind the soup.

'Only those not on welfare and really in need get a bowl. It's not easy to convince them, as you can see.' Father Ota laughed. 'These are our day labourers, and this is their soup kitchen. We supply them with the rice and everything else, but they do the cooking.' Father Ota stepped forward into the room, offering greetings and went to speak with the men who wielded the ladles. Kate felt suddenly conspicuous standing in the doorway, a lone foreign woman, as many turned to look at her. A man nearby slurped loudly, chopsticks shovelling rice and gruel between bristly unkempt jaws. Like so many of the men in the room, he appeared prematurely aged.

'Who are they?' she asked.

'I told you,' he said, 'day labourers. Kamagasaki is a town of day labourers, forty-two thousand of them living on half a square kilometre. That at least is the number registered, but what the figure really is, nobody knows. Most don't register, you see, they prefer to disappear. And this is the place to disappear. There are two other areas like this in Japan, one is Sanya in Tokyo and the other Kotobuki in Yokohama, but Kamagasaki is by far the largest. These men are the exploited workforce behind the whole of Japanese industry.' Father Ota spoke brusquely, opening the door back into the room of envelopes.

'Look,' he said and took her to a map on the wall, pointing out an area cut up and bounded by main roads and railway lines.

'This is Nishinari Ward, Kamagasaki is this corner of it here, although you won't find the name on this map. It's thought better to ignore us. Once the whole area went under the name Kamagasaki, and that's the way we still think of it. I'm afraid we Japanese are given to selective vision, we see only what we want to. We have an inherent sense of beauty, but prefer not to see ugliness. This area is notorious. Its history goes back more than four hundred years. Originally it was a graveyard and place where criminals were executed. In 1615 the Tokugawa Shogunate gave permission to build cheap lodging houses. That was the beginning of the Kamagasaki slums. It's always been a crime infested area of destitutes. The modern Kamagasaki with its exploited day labourers took its present shape with the Korean war.' Father Ota pointed to another corner of the map.

'Nishinari is divided into several areas, it's all very poor. In this part live many dropouts, people who can't fit into society for one reason or another. This block here belongs to the rag pickers. Then this is the gangsters division, nobody goes there, nor the quarter next to it, Tobita, a red light area of prostitution controlled by the gangsters.' Father Ota drew his finger over the map, prodding here and there to define a place.

'Here again is Kamagasaki with its day labourers, and this is the Burakumin quarter. You must know about the Burakumin. They're Japan's untouchables. Even in this day and age they're bitterly discriminated against. Originally, they were tanners of hide and grave-diggers, and lived on the outskirts of all towns. Nobody knows how long their area dates back. Then just over here, beyond Kamagasaki, that's where the Koreans are congregated. They are also a hated non-class here. As you can see, this is the dustbin of society. I don't know how you found us here. Few people come looking for us, and few can find us when they do. Although as you can see, we're situated in the very middle of Osaka, bounded by respectability on all sides. I suppose we're something like a black hole. A sudden step into nothingness.'

'Where is Namba?' Kate stared at the map.

'Namba? It would be just about here; see, that is Namba station.'

Kate followed the roads on the map trying to determine where she might have jumped from Tamura's car. The narrow alleys through which she had run the night before stretched out on the wall before her, now in an innocuous design. She remembered the little curtained doorways and the rows of waiting slippers and shuddered now again.

'Are you all right?' Father Ota observed, with his gentle smile,

Kate nodded but knew she owed him some explanation. This was a place without deceit and where the concentration of most lives was far more bitterly distilled than hers. She might for a time wish to disappear, but there was little she needed to hide, she should tell Father Ota about herself.

'I was there last night.' She pointed to the red light area. 'I think I had a narrow escape.'

Father Ota shifted his weight in concern, and Kate hurried to reassure him, explaining then, as simply as she could, all he might need to know. But she mentioned nothing of her marriage, and as she expected he asked no questions.

'Well, I don't think I've had a runaway of quite your sort before. I don't even know if I should keep you,' he said, his wide face puckered in anxiety.

'I phoned my friends last night, as you know. It's all right. I can't face going back just yet for many reasons. Maybe tomorrow. Please let me stay, I could help you; there must be work you could give me to do. Those envelopes for instance.' She pleaded like a child, sitting down before the stack of paper, determined. Father Ota shook his head, perplexed, but gave her a pile of printed matter and showed her how to fold them the sheet of paper.

'But I can't take responsibility for you beyond tomorrow. It will be my duty then to contact your people. I can see you've got more trouble than you're telling me,' he said shrewdly. 'But I'll give you the benefit of the doubt if it helps you, until tomorrow.'

She picked up an envelope in relief. She had not known she wanted to stay, until the words collected and left her. Her thoughts were slow and without the comfort of a plan. Her real life seemed far away, as if viewed through the wrong end of a telescope. An old man coughed at the table, another slurped his tea. Father Ota's balding head reflected the sun that pushed through the dusty pane of a window. From the other room came the clank of a ladle and the voices of the men. She did not know what destiny had brought her to this depressing place, nor what made her shape the words that asked to remain. She was surprised but accepting of the space that stretched before her now. And tomorrow she would think again.

'Tell me,' she said, 'more about this area. How long have you been here?'

'About ten years. We are several different religious groups here now, working together in an ecumenical way. But we need more volunteers, as we need more of everything here. It's difficult to get outside help or interest, so we try and rehabilitate those we can from the community and train them to help the others, like the men you saw in the soup kitchen, or around this table. On the physical level our main problems here are alcoholism and T.B.. In this day and age there is little T.B. in the rest of Japan, but in Kamagasaki there is hardly a man untouched. And alcoholism, well, this is a town of alcoholics.' The man beside Kate sucked his bowl of tea and asked where to find more envelopes. His voice was hoarse as a wire scourer.

'Now he,' said Father Ota, 'has a story. Once he was a gangster of some responsibility, who fell into disrepute with his gang. He came to us here for help in a desperate state, he too was an alcoholic. You can hear how liquor has ruined his voice. He stayed, was cured of the bottle, and is now very active for us here. A kind of story we don't get very often.'

'Didn't the gang try and get him back?' asked Kate.

'Yes indeed, very few escape as he did. He has now lived peacefully here with us some years, and is one of our main supports.'

'But I don't understand, who are these men, how do they get here, why can't they leave? Why doesn't anyone do anything? Kate asked, bewildered still by the place. 'Why is it a secret?'

Father Ota scratched his head, wondering where he should begin. 'Unlike the rest of unskilled labour in Japan, these men work without contracts, by the day. They work in the most dangerous situations with no security in case of accidents. They're employed on very low wages, the lowest in the hierarchy of labouring classes.

Each morning, hundreds of buses and trucks come into Kamagasaki, organised by the gangs, to pick up the men and take them off, often to far away places. Most of the big construction companies are owned by the gangs. Then there are the loan sharks, who come in cars to pick up the left over men, at lower wages still. Sometimes they are forced to work and are never even paid.

The men live in flophouses or they sleep on the streets. This is a town of single men without families, without women. They have no normal human relationships; they live in loneliness and fear. Once they come here they never get out. Nobody leaves Kamagasaki, except by way of death. And that goes for the whole of this area. You're marked for the rest of society, once it's known you have lived here. You are an outcast for life; no decent job is open to you. Many have tried to leave. Few can ever do it. Sooner or later they all come back.'

'But how do the men get here in the first place, they must have had families at some time?' Kate asked.

'They come by many different routes. Some come to disappear for one personal reason or another. As you know, Japan is a hard place to live in if you don't conform, or lose your place, or suffer shame. Perhaps some have been confined in institutions. Here you need not be ill to be institutionalised, you need only be a nuisance. Many though are poor farmers and fishermen from distant parts, forced to seek work away from home due to our rapid economic growth. They come here thinking they'll take temporary work, to send money home quickly until they find stable jobs. They think they'll soon send for their families. It never happens. The work they do is the worst there is, the money low, life insecure. They return to dreadful living conditions, loneliness, exhaustion and bad nourishment. At first they do send money home, but less and less. Soon they're ill or on the bottle, soon they lose contact with their families. They stay here until they die, and that doesn't take too long. I've some rounds to do this morning. Do you want to come with me? It'll give you some idea of things?'

They walked down the street, which now appeared deserted.

'Except for the old and the sick, you don't see many men at this time. The buses come early and clear the area.' Father Ota explained.

'First I have to go in here, I've been told that someone is sick.' He nodded towards a dilapidated building that displayed a sign that said "hotel". They entered through a glass door into a tiled foyer. There was a strong smell of urine, disinfectant and despair.

Beyond the bare entrance and a reception window in a wall, they faced graffiti, damp cement and metal railings on the stairs. On some dark landings a communal sink with many taps was placed along a wall. At one an old man, bent and bearded, naked to the waist, hawked and spat as he cleaned his teeth. Water ran from his beard like rain from coarse straw. There were many doors along each corridor, stacked like the half-doors of horse-boxes, one upon another, a ladder reached to upper halves. Some were open and Kate saw inside each a rush matted shelf, little bigger than a man. The boxes appeared without light or ventilation.

'This is one of the cheaper *doya*, or flophouses. A man rents a shelf for the night,' Father Ota told her.

Reaching forward, he pulled back a lower door, put in a hand and switched on a light in an odour-filled space. 'There's a light bulb in here, he's lucky.'

The man stirred on his bed and drew himself up on an elbow, his sweaty face hammered by years of drink. His voice rasped like drying glue.

'I'm not a corpse yet, Father Ota, that you must come looking for me. But it's the child here that worries me.' Beside him then Kate saw a bundle under the quilt. A child of three or four with dark and unkempt hair sat up, and slowly rubbed her eyes.

'Is she sick too?' Father Ota asked. The man shook his head.

'No, not sick, but she's not eaten for a couple of days. I don't know how long I've laid here sick. Someone gave her some biscuits last night.' He lay back as Father Ota knelt beside in the tiny cell, examining him and asking further questions.

'I'm taking the child with me; we'll look after her. And I'm calling an ambulance for you. I'll come by and see you again tomorrow in the hospital.' Father Ota lifted the child up in his arms, and stepped back into the corridor beside Kate. The man murmured his thanks and closed his eyes again.

'Her name is Tomoko,' Father Ota said, ruffling the child's mated hair affectionately, producing a sweet from his pocket and giving it to her to eat. They walked back down the dank stairs, Father Ota carrying the docile child.

'We've someone who will take care of her,' Father Ota said over his shoulder.

'How does that man have a child like this? I thought you said they were all single?' Kate asked hurrying to catch up.

'Some strike up with the casual women about, mostly prostitutes, sometimes they try and live as a family. Usually it breaks down, most of the women walk out and leave the man if there's a child. We've had it before. There are many children like this here, left alone on the roads or in those cupboards all day. We do what we can at our children's centre.'

The child gazed at Kate, her dark eyes impenetrable as she bumped along upon Father's Ota's shoulder.

The road was broad and passed a cavernous building open to the road. Father Ota jerked his head towards it.

'That's the depot where the trucks and buses come each morning to pick up the men.'

The huge vaulted interior was empty but for an abandoned bus or two. A few cars were parked about the periphery with labels on their windscreens indicating the place and hours of work and the payment for each day. Knots of men stood about, several of the cars held sullen, waiting passengers. Some men were arguing before a brown station wagon. Inside the car two passengers pressed their faces to the window. The quarrelling grew louder until, kicking and yelling, one of the man was picked up by the others and thrust into the waiting car like a squawking bird. The door was shut firmly upon him, and the car with its captives drove off. Father Ota shook his head sadly. 'Sometimes they press gang them like that. But we can't interfere, we can't meddle with the gangs, otherwise we wouldn't be here. Our work is with the basic life these men go out from and come back to.' Father Ota watched the car drive away; he had seen such things before.

Soon they reached the childcare centre and left Tomoko there, in a cramped room with a kindly woman, and ten other children.

'I've work to do the other side of the ward, if you're not up to the walk, I'll take you back first,' Father Ota said, but Kate shook her head, and they walked on.

They passed a small patch of wasteland hemmed in by a low wall and a few limp trees. Dirty flophouses ringed the square. Father Ota walked by a few old tyres half buried in the ground, and protruding like the humps of a serpent, waiting for children to come and play. Underfoot the ground was a mess of litter, broken bottles and drink cans. The charred pits of dead fires spotted the place, ash blew up into the air. Some filthy quilts were piled in a corner against a wall and Father Ota marched across to poke amongst them, disturbing a sleeping man who shouted incoherently when prodded by the priest.

'He's just drunk,' Father Ota said straightening up in relief. 'I thought he might be ill. I found a man dead in this square just the other day.'

A few elderly residents huddled together. All were swaddled in several layers of clothes belted together with string. Father Ota observed them and sighed.

'In the year we reckon to pick up off the streets several hundred dead. It's the winter that kills them. We go round the streets then each night with blankets, medicine and food.'

Kate looked at him aghast, 'Why doesn't anyone do anything?' Father Ota shrugged and seemed disinclined to talk.

Soon they entered a shopping arcade, that Kate recognised from the night before. She hurried along by Father Ota's side and in the daylight saw that the arcade was indistinguishable in character and content from any other: the butcher, the baker, the chemist, a fish shop and some mundane boutiques. A few bars, a supermarket and a *pachinko* parlour. Some fruit looked dubious in quality, but that was all to note. Father Ota read her thoughts.

'Kamagasaki is rough and grimy, but in parts like this you wouldn't know this area was different from others. You couldn't tell by appearances where you were. And as with everything in Japan, it's appearances that count.' Kate again noticed the elderly women, as she had the night before, standing vacantly about the arcade.

'You always find them here. They're old ex-prostitutes and now they pimp for other women,' Father Ota said in answer to her question, and then drew her attention to the number of leather shops.

'Many people come here to buy cheap leather. This arcade runs through the Burakumin area. They're Japan's answer to India's untouchables, they are our invisible race. They've always dealt in hide. Traditionally they were considered unworthy of the words 'human being', because they lived by blood and death and dirt, things that Shintoism and Buddhism would have no part of. Every defiling trade was theirs, and still is. They did anything no one else would do and paid a price in human rights. They live nowadays by many other trades, and they appear no different from any other modern Japanese. But they are still Burakumin, an unsolved social problem. They have no place in society and live in separate ghettoes. Here they have their own school, they're discriminated against in normal schools. It is impossible for them to marry outside their community or to hold jobs in reputable firms.'

'Who's to know where they come from or who they are. Surely there are ways they could infiltrate society?' Kate asked surprised, looking down the narrow lanes off the arcade at a huddle of little wooden houses, washing lines and open gutters. These were the streets she had run through unknowingly the night before. Father Ota stopped at a fruit shop and bought some oranges.

'Those are Burakumin lanes, they seem normal, until you go into the houses and hear the stories. They cannot infiltrate society because, as you know in Japan, it's impossible to hide a background. Everyone has a detailed family register kept at the Ward Office, that is the mark of being a Japanese. To be struck off the family register is the worst thing that can happen to you. No kind of business hires anybody without a detailed check on backgrounds, no marriage happens without the same thorough check. Pedigree is everything here, sooner or later things come out.

But slowly, very slowly, things are changing I suppose, even here. We're becoming more aware. A lot of idealistic young people now take more interest in these issues.

Now, there is a road here we shall have to cross. But you need not worry, you're safe with me. There's no danger just walking through here. And there is no other way.'

She saw then that it the same road of seedy brothels she had been trapped in the night before, the doors of the small houses were still open, slippers still waiting. The entrances were devoid now of the old women, waiting to welcome customers. In the morning light everything appeared different and subdued. The street was empty with nobody in sight.

'You're quite safe with me. I am known everywhere here,' Father Ota assured her. 'You must forget about last night. Besides, the area is asleep, no one is about at this time.'

And when Kate looked she found she could not even determine now which was the house she had run into. Today it was a different place, sterile in the sun.

'This area is called Tobita, it was the equivalent of the old Yoshiwara in Tokyo,' explained Father Ota, 'and its history is as old, it's been here hundreds of years. Do you know the poor girls in those houses are rarely allowed out, they can sit in the porch or at a window, but that's usually as far as they get. Those girls are different from the bar hostesses or other prostitutes, who although victimised by the gangs have a different status. These girls are the last rung of the prostitution ladder, and the gangs control it all.'

Nobody would ever guess thought Kate looking about, that this was a street of brothels. The houses were poor but neatly kept, with traditional tiled roofs and pretty potted plants before the entrance. The narrow alley had been hosed down and was still wet in the morning sun.

'You must eat, you've had nothing yet. Do you like sushi, shall we go in here?' He pointed to a tiny place and entered when she nodded. They sat on stools before a circular counter, behind which stood a cook with his chopping board, seaweed, fish and cold rice. A conveyor belt of little dishes rattled like a miniature train round the counter. Each dish contained a small cake or two of cold rice wrapped in seaweed or crowned with raw fish.

'I must admit that I knew little of Kamagasaki until I was sent here by my mission. As a Japanese I was almost ashamed to say where my parish was, but as a Christian my indignation at the poverty and inhumanity was as great as yours. Now my work and life is here.

'Some time ago there was a song about Sanya, which is the Kamagasaki of Tokyo. It was called "The Sanya Blues" and had a line in it which went something like, if there were no men in Sanya, no buildings would be built in Tokyo, and we would not be economically where we are today.' Father Ota sighed.

They left the sushi restaurant and continued on under a railway bridge, passing makeshift homes fashioned from cardboard boxes, large crates and old sofas, and soon entered yet another narrow street. At one corner was a large three-storeyed building. The ground floor was open to the road and its entrance filled with a massive slab of superbly grained wood, mounted on a stand. Behind this screen stood incongruously, a black and gleaming Rolls Royce. Opposite the building was a parking place in which waited several large imported cars.

'This road cuts through the gangsters' area, and that building is the headquarters of one of the gangs,' Father Ota nodded to the Rolls Royce. They walked on and were soon free of the road.

They crossed a further beaten looking square, where more heaps of filthy quilts could be seen, and where a man slept in a disused pipe, and another in a large rusty pram. A tramp searched for lunch in a garbage bin, and Father Ota stopped to direct him to the mission's soup kitchen.

'Some of the men here come from decent backgrounds, you know, they're not all lower class. Many come here to escape some personal disaster. I've known disgraced businessmen and others who were alcoholics and so disowned in shame by their families. Everyone has a story.' Father Ota sighed.

The oranges were eventually deposited with an ancient, palsied woman who slept alone in a filthy room on the second floor of a disused warehouse occupied by twenty families. A smell of drains and urine oozed from the place. The woman lay lethargically on a mat. From old sepia photographs on the walls of the room, men in army uniforms and women in kimono stared down at her. Kate placed the fruit upon a dish, and immediately the room had new life, and the woman turned her head to smile at them.

Father Ota stopped at a community house for the elderly, the object of his excursion, to discuss a matter of importance. Kate waited by a window absorbed by the sight outside of a makeshift place of worship before a blackened wall. Three white chrysanthemums had been placed in a whisky bottle, and some incense sticks pushed into a plastic cup of ash. Kate stared at the sight and could not explain the tears that came suddenly to her eyes.

'One more stop,' said Father Ota, 'and then we will return.' He unlocked a green door in a shed-like building and entered a deserted office to collect two files from a drawer.

'Have a look in here,' he said. Kate followed him into the room beyond the office.

It was as if the debris of a jumble sale had been piled into the room, shelves crammed with a bric-a-brac of discarded objects. Everything from children's toys and knitting needles to egg cups and glass marbles filled the shelves, and everything was small in scale. Tiny plastic dolls, building blocks, teacups from a toy house, scissors, knives, photo frames, plastic flowers and stuffed birds. The room was dark and windowless, illuminated only by a bar of fluorescent light on the ceiling

'This is our play therapy room. I've no need to explain the degree of emotional disturbance here amongst residents. One way or another we do a lot of counselling. A certain type of case benefits from this kind of therapy. We have several qualified volunteers working with us here,' Father Ota walked into the middle of the room and pointed to a row of shallow troughs standing on small tables.

'Each one of these trays represents a person's emotional landscape, you know.'

Kate came and stood beside him, staring down at the strange arrangements. The trays were filled with sand in which was planted a haphazard world, constructed with bits and pieces taken from the brimming shelves. These landscapes of the mind stared up at Kate from their narrow containers, Garish naked dolls, glass light bulbs, silk flowers, cars, toy houses and ladders, plastic spiders and broken bottles formed bizarre and muddled worlds.

'The landscapes get more orderly as they improve, if they improve. These are very troubled people.' Father Ota said, turning back towards the door.

Kate followed, but then stopped before another of the boxes. There was no sand in this tray. It was bare and empty to its blue painted bottom, swept clean with such care that not a grain of sand remained. There was nothing in the tray except a ring of grey pebbles placed carefully at the centre. Upon this rested a small metal bowl filled with water, like a pond. An intricately patterned green rock had been placed in the middle of the water, and upon it rested a single fresh daisy. Kate stood before the stark purity of this image, and it held her with strange force. Tears filled her eyes.

'Come,' Father Ota said quietly. 'It is time to go back.'

She nodded, her throat constricted with emotion. Looking up she saw in his expression an understanding of everything she had not told him. His eyes, behind their bottle thick lenses, viewed the world without accusation. He held the door open and she passed him quickly, wiping her tears away.

22

The envelopes now filled the table in untidy piles, addressed to a shadowy mass of names who might care to read them or might not. Father Ota came into the room from the outer office.

'There's someone to see you.'

Kate put down an envelope looking up in alarm. Father Ota nodded and smiled encouragement. Following him into the other room, she was sure she would find her husband waiting there. Instead of Jun, Pete stood in Father Ota's office, and relief flooded through her. Father Ota left them together, shutting the door behind him.

'I never thought I'd find you. I've been wandering round this place for hours, trying to trace you,' Pete said in a conversational way. Kate stared blankly at him.

'I always thought foreigners were so conspicuous here, but nobody seems to have seen you, except for a fruit shop in an arcade. They said you stopped there with that missionary. Finally, it was an old tramp I did not think worth asking who brought me here. God, what a place.'

He did not tell her of his queries at the houses with the slippers, but waited before her with his quiet smile. She looked down silently at her hands as she sat on a chair.

'We were worried,' he added. She nodded silently, and did not ask how he knew she was here in Kamagasaki.

He was out of place in the room, the cut and colour of his raincoat carrying with it a world from which she was now far removed. It seemed a long while since she had seen him; she had entered another dimension. She tried to think of Kobe, of Itsuko and Jun, of Paula. Her thoughts moved over these things like thin clouds blown by the wind. She gripped the metal frame of the chair beneath her, and looked up at Pete in confusion. He sat down beside her and took her hand as if she was a child.

'I want you to come back with me. I'm not here for myself, Jun has sent me, he knew you were here. That missionary says you want to stay a bit longer, and I can understand your confusion, but I think you should return.'

'Then why didn't Jun come himself?' She looked up sharply, something breaking in her.

'It's difficult to explain. A lot has happened. The reasons he has not come are not what you think.'

He told her then of the complications Tamura had evolved for Jun. Pressing her gently for details of all that had happened since they last met, relieved to hear things were not as Tamura had indicated in his letter to Jun; the man had no hold upon them.

'The past can be the past if you want,' he said. 'It is no more than memory, and what is memory but a thought. The future can be different. I think Jun only sought to protect you from things he himself did not know how to cope with.'

'Then he must tell me so himself,' she said, hardening her voice to cover her emotions.

She could not so easily appear to forgive everything that had passed. There was that child and there was Itsuko, her face encrusted with a smile of malice that nothing would dissolve. Yet, even as these thoughts came to her, she saw again in her mind the small, blue tray she had stood before earlier in the day. Nothing could explain the feelings that it left within her. The bare tray, the careful pebbles and clear water, the daisy on the rock; a hope so pure and strong that it lived forever, separate from the broken life that made it. She drew a breath and looked at Pete. Compared to that broken life, there was so much she saw now in her own to salvage.

Even as she spoke she was filled with fatigue. Itsuko appeared like an old ivory queen on a chessboard, calling checkmate to the world. With an effort she put the thought aside.

'If he wishes to prove our life together still holds some meaning, he must come and tell me. I know this is an ugly place, but I can see some true perspectives from here. They're always in need of volunteers, they won't mind if I stay.'

He saw she shivered with emotion, her hands clenched tightly before her.

'Wait,' she whispered and left the room in search of paper and a pen.

Climbing the ladder stairs, she sat upon the bed, and began a letter to Jun, placing words on the paper, without emotion. Each word as it formed beneath her hand seemed to anchor events about her again, like scenery on a stage set for an act that was yet to be played, while she waited in the wings. She wished Pete had never found her. It was enough to support her own emotions, without those of other people. She folded the letter, placed it in an envelope and wrote Jun's name upon it.

23

Itsuko turned a rice paper page of the hand-bound book upon her lap. The language of *Noh* was medieval, and she had brought with her to the theatre her own modern translation of the play. Upon the stage three musicians on folding stools waited for the audience to settle. There was silence and then a strange, inarticulate, deep-throated cry from the man with a long drum held to his shoulder. The sharp crack and the hollow thud of the drums wound in between an eerie flute. Itsuko closed her eyes and let the sounds lead her to their timeless world.

She never missed the first *Noh* performance of the season, and today she could relax a little for she was sure the stress of the last few days would soon be behind her. At the insistence of the detectives she had written to Tamura, asking for more time to deliver the blueprints. Kate was not yet found in that disreputable area, although discreet inquiries had been made at innumerable dubious houses there. But the detectives had confirmed that Kate had escaped, and it appeared Tamura's threats were mostly bluff. She would see Tamura finished for this; she would see to it that he got jail instead of her blueprints.

The chanting of the chorus brought her back to the performance.

Before her, the apron stage was devoid of scenery but two large wooden columns indicating the entrance to a shrine. Three small living pine trees stood along the entry ramp, representing heaven, earth and man. The immaculate polished stage was austere, but brilliant with light.

Jun moved impatiently in his seat beside his mother. He found *Noh* difficult at the best of times, and even more so today. He had not told his mother that Kate had been found and was safe. According to Pete, Tamura had nothing but groundless threats of spite. Relief made Jun light-headed. Soon he would go to bring Kate back, but until that moment he wished to hold the knowledge secret within him, like her letter in his pocket. She would come back, he knew it now. And he would prove to her that he was not as she thought. They would have a different life now; it was not too late. He had already made that clear to Chieko.

On this day each year he always accompanied his mother to the *Noh*, as his father had done before him. It was one of her few real pleasures. They always came in the morning. The performance was long, eight hours or more, divided into five or six plays. His mother did not like to miss *Okina*, that old and ritual play with which the performance always began. It was a play without a plot, it was the dedication of the mask to the mystery of divinity. The theatre of *Noh* was not a mirror of life, but an image in the mirror to which life approximates. Like a form of meditation, the effort through *Noh* was to transcend time.

It annoyed Itsuko to enter the theatre halfway through the day, into the middle of performances, but with the detectives and the worry of Tamura, this had been unavoidable. Jun was relieved to have only to endure two hours of *Noh* for he would also leave early. Pete was to meet him here at the theatre;

his office was nearby in Osaka. They were going together to Kamagasaki. It would be a shock to Itsuko, but that was as Jun planned. It was better that way, she would have no time to think or forestall him. He had considered going without informing her but that would bring its problems. Knowing already where Kate was, it had been difficult to listen to the useless suggestions of the detectives earlier through the morning.

On the stage the chorus sat with their fans on the floor before them. An actor advanced with measured, sliding steps to the centre of the stage. He was masked and rotundly wrapped in many layers of heavy brocade kimono. The chorus informed them that this was the beautiful daughter of Kino Aritsune. Beneath the ethereal mask, protruded the jowls of an elderly man. For long periods he stood totally still or circled the stage in a protracted way, while the chorus chanted hypnotically. Jun could not seem to break through the static actions and find the experience beyond. He could not concentrate for long enough to pass through the eye of the needle and into the impenetrable *Noh*, but slid from its surface like rain from a leaf. Today he impatiently watched a somnambulist's world, of remote mannered postures and sequences. He looked at his watch and tried again to narrow his thoughts to the play, all that filled his mind was Kate, and his own nervous anticipation. Beside him his mother appeared to have crossed the moat of white pebbles, separating everyday life from the distant world of the stage.

A strange peace always took hold of Itsuko when she came to the *Noh*, a feeling she rarely recaptured elsewhere. For a fleeting moment she had no wish to seem in life quite the predator she appeared. But that was her role and responsibility, a destiny that was impossible to reject. The cast of fate was always hard, as was apparent on the stage before her. Each play was the exploration of a state of emotion through the personification of a departed soul. Now, on the stage, was the outline of a well, just an open wooden framework and a spray of pampas grass. This was the play, *Izutsu*, the story of the nobleman poet Narihira and Kino Aritsune's daughter. Itsuko's eyes followed the thickly garbed actor, prayer beads in one hand, a bunch of green leaves in the other. The mask was secured by purple ribbons at the back of a straight, black wig. He reached the middle of the stage and the voice when it came from behind the mask was a muffled and fossilised thing, a sound thrown up from a distant place.

> Every dawn in the offering water
> The moon too, sinks in reflection,
> Her soul calm and clear ...

The flat words grew facets and depths and touched her. Then the strange esoteric ballet with its barest economy of movement and sound, became a distillation of all human emotion, and tears filled her eyes. For this was *yugen*, the essence of *Noh*.

With her husband, this love of *Noh* was the only thing they had seemed to share. They had always come together, this first day of the season. Itsuko remembered still the beauty of the words with which he had explained to her the depth and meaning of *yugen*.

It is a place, he had told her, of eternal truth. Everything fades, life, beauty and happiness. The soul passes on alone and desolate. *Yugen* is universal loneliness. *Yugen* is the soul of *Noh*.

She remembered the way he had looked at her then, with tenderness she could never again recall. She was sure that it was on that night Jun had been conceived. She swallowed hard to force back the tears that filled her eyes again. She felt old and very tired.

The world of silence had caught Jun now, and drew him briefly in. The ghost of Kino Aritsune's daughter changed into the robes of her dead lover and danced, half-man, half-woman, an ancient court hat on her head, in a kimono of gold and purple. It was a dance almost without movement, a solemn circling of the stage, frozen but flowing, effortless but erect, an unearthly, beautiful thing.

> The voice of the pines murmurs in the wind,
> Its course elusive, ever shifting,
> Such in life is the dreambound soul,
> At what sound will it awaken?

The words deposited him in a strange, bare land. It no longer mattered that beneath the mask was an aging man, or that his hands were wide and gnarled. They faded until only his soul remained, expressing its torment and bittersweet longing. He communicated an eternity it was thought no young woman could portray. And the mask in its stillness evoked more than the most expressive face, changing gently as the shadows moved, from poignancy into grief.

At last the actor came to the well, and knelt in the final moments of the play, gazing down at the reflection on the water of the moon and Narihira's ghostly image. The words and gestures fell in and out of time.

Nothing happens, but memory
Long clings in this earthly life.

The plantain leaves rustle,
Broken easily as dreams.

The dream is broken, and it is day.

The play reached its consummation in the strange residue of silence that filled the audience and the stage as the last words faded away. No one moved for several moments. The words came to Jun like an eerie portent of everything that had been, and everything that might yet come. He swallowed at a sudden fear that gripped him from within. Then the audience stirred, pushing away the bare realm that had held them all captive. He sighed in relief and looked at his watch, it was the intermission, and time for him to leave Itsuko and go to Kate. Pete would be at the entrance soon.

Jun steered his mother out of the auditorium and towards the refreshment kiosks. He found Itsuko a place on a bench and brought her green tea, a sugared bean cake and three tangerines in a small net bag. He knew he must find the words to tell her now. Already Pete was visible at the door, his head above the crowd, Jun caught his eye and nodded to him to wait.

Itsuko bit fastidiously into the bean cake, chewing slowly to decide its worth. She noticed the expression on Jun's face and looked up at him in question. He shifted his weight from one foot to the other.

'I have found Kate. Pete went for me to Kamagasaki, she is safe at a Christian mission. Tamura has nothing on us, I'm sorry,

I should have told you this morning. I'm going to bring Kate back. Pete is already at the theatre, ready to go with me. I must do what I feel is right for myself, and for Kate. I don't want to disturb this afternoon for you. I'll just leave quietly now.'

Itsuko lowered the bean cake, and swallowed abruptly. 'This is not the right way. It is good she is safe, certainly. I am glad for us all. But you must not go. We are not yet sure we are clear of Tamura. Let Bailey-*san* go, as before. Let him keep her, as before, in his home, until we can decide what to do with her, what is best.' Itsuko raised the bean cake again to her lips, and took a determined bite.

His heart beat fast. He should have gone without telling her. She had not even thought of Kate returning to her role as his wife. He saw now how she would use Kate's desertion to force his marriage to an end. She did not care about his feelings, much less about Kate's. She had not thought once that things could mend.

Outside the auditorium, people talked and ate. An old couple beside Itsuko crunched loudly on rice crackers and slurped green tea. Itsuko waited silently, taking a tangerine from the bag, ignoring the possibility that anything more need be asked or answered. She began to peel the fruit and refused to look at Jun. The sharp smell of the tangerine rose up to him as she broke into the flesh.

Through the open doors of the auditorium the stage rose bare and blond above the moat of dim seats. He saw now that his life lay forked before him with a choice he had wished not to see. He thought back to that time in London, when he had lived with Kate above Holland Park, and it seemed from here like a past incarnation, already many lives removed. He remembered that party at the Baileys, where he had first met Kate. He remembered how, after a visit to *Romeo and Juliet*, he had explained the popularity in Japanese literature of the theme of double suicide.

He looked down upon Itsuko's sculptured head bowed above the tangerine, and knew at last the choice he must make to free himself to his own life. The virtues he had inherited at birth and that made him Japanese would always return him firmly to duty, and his place in an inflexible order of things. He saw then all he must relinquish if he was to gain. Without a word he turned away from Itsuko, and walked to where Pete waited.

There was a pip in her mouth that lay on her tongue behind her front teeth. As she stared at Jun's departing back, the two remaining tangerines rolled unheeded from her lap. The sweet juice filled her mouth like acid, she could not swallow, could not breathe. Jun had taken leave of his senses; she would never forgive him now. With an effort Itsuko swallowed the mouthful of juice and inadvertently also the pip. Turning her head, blinking back tears of frustration, Itsuko stared through the open door of the auditorium to the empty, solitary world of the stage. She sat, unmoving, her face convulsed and old, clutching the concave shell of peel that was all that remained of her tangerine.

Someone nudged her shoulder gently. A woman returned with a smile the string bag with two tangerines that had rolled from her lap. Itsuko stood up, she moved slowly back towards the auditorium and the enigmatic stage. Sitting down again in her seat, she, found the page in her book for the next play.

24

The sick of Kamagasaki were a nuisance and a liability, and alcoholic besides. Father Ota told Kate as he hurried along after they left the medical centre, 'If we visit them in the hospital and the staff see we have an interest in them, sometimes they will keep them in for a little while longer. However, most men who are really ill just resign themselves to death. Some, like our runaway friend, Tomoko's father, discharge themselves, much to the hospital's relief, but if they do that more than once, they're blacklisted and cannot be admitted again.'

The sick man in the flophouse who they had visited the day before, and whose child they had taken to the children's centre, had discharged himself from hospital just before their arrival. They walked in the afternoon sun and Kate breathed deeply, thankful to be out of the place with its smells of distress and antiseptic.

'We must find him, he's ill,' Father Ota continued. 'The first place he'll go after discharging himself from hospital, is to pick up his child, and then there's no knowing where he'll disappear to. Even when they know we're from the church, it's sometimes still difficult for these men to trust us. They always think we're going to tell the police and have them put away.' Father Ota walked purposefully along.

After Pete had left the day before, Kate had told Father Ota everything. He had listened quietly, nodding his head sympathetically.

'I can understand your difficulties. Our society is not an easy one. Like you, the church too has a hard time here in Japan. If it is any comfort to you, in a way our problems are somewhat like yours. Sometimes its seems difficult to be both a good Christian and a good Japanese. Godliness here is a love of finitude, a training in efficiency and self-reliance whose rewards are here and now.

'And how have you settled your dilemma?' she had asked him in amusement.

He smiled and shook his head, unwilling to reply. 'It's a constant battle, never quite decided, I suppose. I try my best to be first a good Christian, which means I am often not a very good Japanese. No, in fact, many people think I'm a very odd man indeed.' He laughed, and it did not seem to worry him.

'You must go back, you must try again, there will be a way.' In the dying light of the silent room he had leaned forward towards her earnestly, a good and honest man, his vision clear and simple as the realities he saw.

'The only condition in life that we can depend upon is change. Change is growth, and you cannot hold back from all that must mature you.' He advised.

'And what have you decided?' he asked as they walked along.

'I shall take your advice. I'll go back. Jun will come, I know. And the fact that I know that, means we already have a new beginning. That already we have found a way.'

'We cannot know what light is if we have never known darkness. But, as in a day, neither light nor darkness lasts forever, but give way to each other repeatedly. Everything has its purpose.' Father Ota nodded.

They turned into a main road that bounded one side of Kamagasaki. Here Father Ota stopped at the door of the medical centre in the hope that the runaway man might be there. Through a window Kate glimpse a few dejected-looking old men.

'I'll wait out here,' she told Father Ota, not wanting to enter yet another place for the sick or rejected.

She felt warm within her jacket, walking along a little further, to be rid of the window of old men. Already in the morning she had come along this stretch of road with Father Ota on his errands. She had not noticed the entrance to the shrine then. It was partly hidden by a short, spreading tree. A small courtyard lay beyond the arch of *torii*, guarded by stone lions, hemmed in by buildings. There was a bell rope and an offertory box before the open doors. She found some *yen* and tossed them in, shook the rope to ring the bell and clapped her hands to summon the gods to her mortal presence. Although only a few steps removed from the road, the shrine was quiet and peaceful. The air was edged with the scents of old stone and wood. Up the steps the interior was dim and empty, a small, bare room of polished boards, silent and austere as the residue of hope and sorrow that rested there. Offerings of rice and fruit and the evergreen *sakaki*, were laid upon the altar. A few pinewood steps ascended to the small latticed door of the innermost chamber of the shrine. Within it the gods rested, invisible to the world. Within that sacred chamber lay only emptiness, and silence.

Kate stood before the shrine and it drew her to into its stillness. She looked up then and saw. On the cross beam above the altar was the symbol of all Shinto shrines, a polished silver mirror resting on a carved wooden cloud. She stared up at it, and it showed her nothing but the reflection of her own face. And that too dissolved and reformed as the flowing colours of the road moved across its surface. And she saw then that, as in the mirror, all thoughts and impressions formed only to dissolve, of no more substance than a dream. The only thing that remained unchanging was the mirror itself on its ethereal cloud. Everything else only came and went in some fleeting dance of time. She turned away then and could not explain the strange peace that seemed to fill her.

'There you are! I was looking for you, Someone just told me our hospital runaway has been found. He's been told to report to me at the mission, and Tomoko will be brought there too,' Father Ota explained in relief as he hurried up to her.

They made their way towards the nearby mission, and passed the labourers' depot again. A heap of broken glass in a gutter reflected in the sun, a shabby window glinted silver. As Kate turned to speak to Father Ota, a child in a pink dress rushed by them.

'It's Tomoko,' Kate exclaimed, trying to catch hold of the child.

At the children's centre, the child had been bathed and dressed in fresh clothes. Her grubby face was now white as magnolia flesh, the hair that was yesterday stiff with dirt fell softly about her small face.

'It's Tomoko,' Kate exclaimed again.

'And there is her father on his way to the mission,' Father Ota said, hailing the man in relief.

The other side of the road Tomoko's father shuffled towards the child, waving to her, his face lighting up at the sight of her. The child gave a shout and turned into the road to run to him. As she reached the middle of the road, a truck turned the corner with a loud swerve of brakes, making for the labourers depot. It was an open-backed truck filled with returning men, all noisy with release from work and an early swig of liquor. The truck careened towards them, and seemed not to see the child crossing, nor hear her father's cry of warning.

It came on towards them all. Kate leapt forwards towards the child. For an instant, the truck towered above her, filling the sky, the reddened faces of the men stared down at her as if from a great height. She reached the child and snatched her up, gripping her hard, and for a moment their bodies clung together, the child's heart moving against her own in astonishment more than fear. Then, flinging the child from her, Kate jumped clear herself of the advancing truck and stood again safely at the side of the road. The vehicle braked with an angry screeching of tyres, and began skidding towards where Kate stood, unprotected. It picked her up and tossed her like a frail reed against a nearby wall. She fell to the road with a soft thud, and lay unmoving there.

It had happened in seconds before he could even cry out a warning. Father Ota stared down at Kate's limp body. They covered her with a blanket brought from the medical centre around the corner, but the doctor knelt and shook his head. The men from the truck stood about in a circle, dazed and subdued. The child and the old man crouched together beside Father Ota who stood silently as the doctor stood up and shook his head once again.

There was a stir then at the back of the crowd. He looked round to see the tall American, who had come to the mission the day before, elbow his way to the front. Beside him was a young Japanese, immaculately dressed in a navy blue suit and an expression of disbelief. It must be the husband, thought Father Ota, and turned resignedly to take his brief part in an act destiny had assigned to him.

25

In the house now silence lay about them. They immersed themselves in activities and little was said.

Itsuko knelt on the veranda, a cushion beneath her knees. The doors of the room were pulled back to the garden, the evenings were cooling and drawing in. Although the sky was still bright the moon was already present and full, white as a mirror above the earth. Itsuko felt considerably exposed. Today was a day in one thousand years when to the West in the pre-dawn sky, eight planets would align. Everywhere people awaited this cosmic climax in dread. Catastrophes were forecast, but nothing had occurred. In the garden, behind the blaze of a maple, Jun lethargically assembled a telescope. Itsuko watched him, her brow knotted as she fanned away a dark, persistent fly. Beside her on the floor the front page of the newspaper showed a photograph of the gathering planets, their names labelled in white upon a black sky. She looked up and thought of them settled there, ageless, timeless and imponderable, glaring down upon her. She felt a touch of terror. Beside the photograph was the article about Kate. Itsuko kept returning to it, unable any longer to remain superior to events. She had never wished for this death. Never. Of that she was innocent, even if for the rest everything was as she had planned. Jun was hers and free again, he would recover from his grief. The newspapers had seen fit to endow Kate's death with missionary zeal, reporting it as a heroic sacrifice to save a child and an example to them all, as she had worked for those less fortunate than herself with Father Ota. The publicity had centred a more positive interest upon Kamagasaki. The Nagai name had emerged fortified, rather than diminished. No more had been heard of Tamura, there was nothing he could do. Why then did Itsuko find herself trembling, that darkness filled her?

Before her, a five-needled *bonsai* pine waited to begin its training. Itsuko took up her scissors, drew it towards her and began to thin and trim. She had never thought of a death. *Never.* She repeated it firmly to herself, but her hands shook slightly as she massaged the branches of the pine to age its infantile bark. Alive, Kate could be relegated to irritating unimportance. But death transformed her to a threat that bled Itsuko of sleep. She began to snip at the small tree, but her hand trembled again and soon she put down the scissors and picked up a roll of wire. Gently, she pulled errant branches to their destined places, binding them carefully with the wire, so that they would not spring again into the free and uncouth jumble nature had intended. She had never known such fear, and dared not voice it, even to Fumi. Here they lived closely with the spirits and in that form now, Kate had the power to hold Itsuko to ransom. She remembered the ghost stories told to her in childhood, and her mother's fear of bad spirits. If she did not live in these modern times she too, thought Itsuko, might be persuaded to believe in *uri*, those vengeful creatures who died violent and untimely deaths that made it difficult to turn their backs upon the living.

They floated around at night without feet, full of bitterness and malice. There was no end to the terror they wrought. Itsuko swallowed hard. She must not let these infantile fears destroy her. Everyone knew that *uri* were no more than the tales of old women. But her hand still trembled inexplicably when she thought of her vulnerability before such inhuman forces. There was no way she could protect herself.

And they also had to live with disharmony now. There was little worse in a well-balanced life than the horror of disharmony. That break, in order and pattern, that Kate's life and death had imposed upon them would sit like a stain on their family history, impossible to obliterate in the minds of those who knew the truth. Such discords went against the functioning of every ethic Itsuko knew. She shuddered and with an effort brought her attention back to the plant before her.

Carefully, she made the last amendments to the tiny, stunted tree. With extra-fine wire she bound smaller stubborn twigs and straightened shoots so that all the pine needles would face upwards. Then she sat back to judge the effects of imprisonment upon the tree. The wire would be left in place until it bit into the branches. Then for a time the tree was released, only to be bound again as it sought to lose its intended shape. Three wirings were needed before the dwarfed tree made no more effort at deviation. Itsuko brushed loose soil from her hands and pushed the tree away. She breathed deeply to calm herself, and tried not to think of the assembling planets or the invisible Kate, more alive now in death than ever in life.

Fumi drew out a stream of blond thread from a faded cotton bag. Its wooden handles knocked sometimes beneath the crochet hook, moving deftly in her hand. The light was fading in her corner of the veranda. She switched on a lamp and closed the panel of mosquito netting between the open doors. Immediately, a moth appeared to flutter round the light. The dry, ancient smells of the garden stirred her sadly to admit that many memories did not survive beyond a deep feeling in her bones. Life moved on like the thread in her little hook drawn from an infinite bag.

She sighed and looked at Jun behind the maple, setting up the telescope with careless apathy. Nothing in his life she felt, justified the hard and bitter facts. None of it was what he intended; he was not callous, he was not cruel. And Kate. She thought of the unfinished baby clothes she had so recently folded away in the iron-bound chests, and remembered the day she had shown Kate the contents of those chests. She thought of all Kate had undoubtedly suffered and her swift and violent death, and wondered if the rites she had requested the priest to perform in the house and at the local shrine would ever really placate a tormented soul. She would pray, and welcome Kate's spirit back at the next *Obon* with greetings and obeisance. Until then, and especially for the first forty-nine days, until the links of the dead were truly severed with this world and they might go forward freely in their new dimension, Fumi would make offerings each day in the little black lacquer house shrine in her room, of rice and fruit and *sake* wine, to absolve the penitence the living must always feel towards the dead. Only after the rites of the seventh week might Kate, wherever she was, feel a peace Fumi knew she deserved. This was the very least, and sadly now, thought Fumi, the most she could ever do to help.

She looked at Itsuko, determinedly moulding a little tree to a shape she thought she desired, and sighed again pulling more thread from her cotton bag. The patternings that enmeshed them in life were so strange.

She wiped the tears from her eyes for she knew Jun would need her now again.

It had been his father's telescope, a professional, complex one. He had not looked at it for years. He polished the lens and examined it for scratches. The sky was fading and he wondered if the pale star he saw now might be Arcturus or Mars. Fumi and his mother had suggested he resurrect the telescope, as they might offer comfort to a child. It was amazing they could really think he was back here as before. The moon was full and bright, he could not think, he could not feel. How could they be sure he would ever be as he was before because a conflict was removed. He was bound to Kate, as much in death as he had been in life, to the choice he had made when he married her. His mother might pull and bind that little tree, securing it to its determined shape, but he had escaped and could never in spirit be made to fit again. For better or for worse. He was like the *bonsai* that planted once in open ground could never be repotted. He was free inwardly now to spread like the roots of those released trees, refusing forever the fetters that once bound them. Their shapes became unattractive and their balance often lopsided, but they grew as they wished, without restriction or plan, in a way the Universe, not man, had intended.

Kate. He silently whispered her name. The moon above was white and bright as a mirror. He knew then suddenly that for them all, true guilt would now begin.

[A]lso by Meira Chand

The Gossamer Fly

ISBN: 978-981-4828-21-5

Confronted by an arrogant and manipulative new maid after her mother is sent back to England following a breakdown, Natsuko, a young girl of English-Japanese parentage, is thrust into a dark and sinister adult world, causing her to retreat into mounting isolation, confusion, fear and anger, leading to a dramatic conclusion in this emotionally charged story.

Last Quadrant

ISBN: 978-981-4828-22-2

In the havoc of a great typhoon, Akiko finds herself stranded with Eva, her adoptive mother, Kyo, the natural mother she has never known and Daniel, a troubled young man who has fallen in love with her. In the brief calm of the typhoon's eye, the group arrives at the comparative safety of their wealthy English neighbour's concrete house. There they must wait out the violence of the last quadrant – the wildest part of the storm. As the refugees draw together in a fight for survival and are forced to reckon with their deepest selves, the terrible night becomes a turning point for each of them.

Sacred Waters

ISBN: 978-981-4779-50-0

Orphaned as a child and widowed at thirteen, Sita has always known the shame of being born female in Indian society. Her life constrained and shaped by the men around her, she could not be more different from her daughter, Amita, a headstrong university professor determined to live life on her own terms. Richly layered and beautifully evocative, the novel is a compelling exploration of two women's struggle to assert themselves in male-dominated societies of both the past and the present.

A Choice of Evils

ISBN: 978-981-4828-24-6

Set against the backdrop of the Sino-Japanese war of the 1930s, the story of those tumultuous years is told through the lives of a disparate group of fictional characters: a young Russian woman émigré caught between her complex love affair with a British journalist and a Japanese diplomat, an Indian nationalist working for Japanese intelligence, a Chinese professor with communist sympathies, an American missionary doctor and a Japanese soldier, all brought together by the monstrous dislocation of war, enmeshed in a savage world beyond their control.

ABOUT THE AUTHOR

Meira Chand is of Indian-Swiss parentage and was born and educated in London. She has lived for many years in Japan, and also in India. In 1997 she moved to Singapore, and is now a citizen of the country. Her multi-cultural heritage is reflected in her novels.

Also by Meira Chand:

A Different Sky

A Far Horizon

House of the Sun

The Painted Cage